Praise for Bill Meissner's
previous short story collection,
HITTING INTO THE WIND
[Random House Publishers]

"Bill Meissner's *Hitting into the Wind* is a quiet masterpiece of baseball writing. These short and revelatory works are rich with poetic language and convincing characters.

—Greensboro, N.C. *News and Record*

"A book....not only for the true baseball fan, but also for the true lover of quality short fiction."

—*Dallas Morning News*

"Meissner's *Hitting into the Wind* captures the essence of baseball, but more important, the essence of fiction itself. This book isn't just good baseball fiction; it's good fiction, period."

—*Bookpage*

"Skillfully using baseball as a metaphor for life, Meissner produces tales that speak of yearning, childhood and dreams... You don't need to be a baseball fan to enjoy these poignant tales."

—*Houston Chronicle*

"Touching, personal tales. Meissner's collection is superb, for both baseball fans and lovers of short stories."

—*Sacramento Bee*

"Meissner...writes less about how the game is played on the field than how it is lived in the heart. He is very good at this, as good as anyone I've ever read. Finely crafted short stories."

—*Boston Sunday Globe*

"His short stories blend the ironic edge of Raymond Carver and the poetic rhythms of Richard Hugo, using baseball as a touch point for life experiences."

—*Los Angeles Times* [syndicated feature]

"Bill Meissner captures baseball with all its crystalline beauty—the remarkable reverberation of time and space and character. These resonant and affecting stories are not baseball stories exactly, but rather stories about men and women, fathers and sons, all connected, in some way, to the summer game."

—*Seattle Post-Intelligencer*
[New York Times Wire Service syndicated article]

"Meissner's tales manage a dreamy, introspective lyricism that's surprisingly winning."

—USA Today

"As in the case in the best sports fiction, the game is usually a pretext for an examination of deeper issues and emotions. For Meissner, baseball is a bulwark against change, against the painful, even tragic evanescence of life itself. The best stories in this collection express that feeling with great tenderness."

—Publisher's Weekly

"This is a beautifully written book of baseball fiction. It is one to be savored, bit by bit, not read in gulps."

—Winston-Salem Journal

"These 30 short stories are about baseball...But they're about more than that. There are characters that tug at the heartstrings."

—Gannett News Service Wire Story

"The stories are fully formed, haunting and beautiful."

—Kirkus Reviews

"A perfect pitch. *Hitting into the Wind* is the confluence of literary imagination and years of playing baseball."

—Minneapolis Star Tribune

"Elegant short stories anchored by a baseball theme..."

—USA Today Baseball Weekly

"Meissner is a must-read for this baseball season and worth keeping around to whet the appetite in the off-season as well. *Hitting into the Wind* is baseball writing at its best."

—Sunday Oklahoman

"For Meissner...time, memory and baseball are interwoven with the most significant and insignificant moments of life. The result...is captivating writing."

—Orlando Sentinel

"Meissner...has a feel for both baseball's appeal and the people to whom it appeals. A lovely book."

—Booklist

LIGHT AT THE EDGE OF THE FIELD

stories by

Bill Meissner

STEPHEN F. AUSTIN STATE UNIVERSITY PRESS

Production Manager: Kimberly Verhines
Editorial Assistant: Katt Noble

IBSN: 978-1-62288-410-0

For more information:
Stephen F. Austin State University Press
P.O. Box 13007 SFA Station
Nacogdoches, Texas 75962
sfapress@sfasu.edu
www.sfasu.edu/sfapress
936-468-1078

Distributed by Texas A&M University Press Consortium
www.tamupress.com

CREDITS AND ACKNOWLEDGMENTS

I am grateful to the following publications where these stories first appeared:

Mid American Review: "The Descending God," "Wing Tip Shoes" (in another form)

Passages North: "El Relampago" Selected by W.P. Kinsella in a fiction contest

Minnesota Monthly: "An Elusive Kind of Light," "Tough Luck Ballplayer in the Diamond Bluff Tavern"

The Road to Cosmos: "The Groundskeeper" and "The Things You Lose" (used by permission, University of Notre Dame Press)

Nine, A Journal of Baseball History and Culture: "The Dreams of Batting Gloves," "End of the Season: Tough Luck Ballplayer in the Diamond Bluff Tavern" (in an earlier version), "Fly Balls With My Father"

Aethlon, A Journal of Sport Literature: "Wing Tip Shoes" (in another form), "Instruction Manual: The Three Things, and One Or Two Others," "What's Missing: The Three Things, and Something Else"

In Other Words: Merida: "The Descending God" (reprinted)

Midwest Quarterly: "The Migration" (portions published in a different form as "Something About Certain Old Baseball Fields") Reprinted in the anthology *Line Drives*

"El Relampago" was chosen by W. P. Kinsella for an award in the *Passages North* fiction competition.

Sections from some of the writings in this collection appear in *CIRCLING TOWARD HOME*, a collection of writings and photos by Bill Meissner. I am grateful to Finishing Line Press for permission to reprint excerpts from the following: "The Things You Lose: An Elusive Kind of Light," "End of the Season: Tough Luck Ballplayer in the Diamond Bluff Tavern," "Circles: The Outfield Dancer," "What's Missing: The Three Things, and Something Else," "Baseball Wife at the Start of the Season," and "The Romance of Certain Abandoned Baseball Fields."

I'd like to extend my thanks to the many friends, writers, and former students who have supported my writing over the years, especially Jack Driscoll, writer extraordinaire. I am also grateful to the dozens of participants in The Catch and Release Baseball Club, a group of pick-up ballplayers that occasionally takes the field, including veteran members Mickey "Mantle" Hatten, Bill "Tater" Kaeter, Ted "Williams" Sherarts, charter member Steve "King of the Diamond" Lyon and founding father Dale "Baseball Buddha" Bailey (RIP). Author Tim O'Brien has remained our most literate participant, and Emmy-winning broadcaster Bob Costas has acted as our absentee celebrity color commentator.

I would like to thank the Loft-McKnight Foundation for an Award of Distinction in Fiction and a Jerome Foundation Travel-Study Grant, which supported the writing of the stories set in Mexico. I am also grateful to the Minnesota State Arts Board and the National Endowment for the Arts for writing fellowships which supported and encouraged my writing.

Finally, a special thanks to my wife, Christine, for her thoughtful comments and suggestions on many of these stories.

This short story collection is a work of fiction. Some locations in the stories are actual places, but the characters and events are fictious.

This book is for Christine and Nathan, with love.
You're always my best teammates, on and off the field.

In memory of my father and mother, Leonard Meissner, and Julia Vavra Meissner,
who made sure I was on the right base paths.

CONTENTS

PART ONE:
THE FIRST PITCH

WHAT'S NEXT: THE BASEBALL LOVERS

1

Ballplayers are hard to figure out, I've always thought. Like the man I love, for instance. Brett never wants to talk about the things I want to talk about. He never wants to talk about the world—about the shape of pears, for instance, or the music of the sunlight angling through the blinds of the window in the morning. He doesn't want to discuss the scars we both might have, and how we feel about them, or about the future, or the distance between our fingertips. I wish he would talk more about those things, but if he doesn't, then I can't be just a ballplayer's girlfriend much longer.

Lately, he only wants to talk baseball: outs, hits, scores, earned run average, as if they're always there, lined up at the very front of his brain and waiting to step out. It's a strange thing for a grown twenty-seven-year-old man to focus on, I think—throwing a small leather ball over a black and white plate, but that's all he seems to think about lately.

What he talks is pitching: the angle of his arm, the way he grips the red stitches. The way he spins the ball with a fast, tight rotation as he lets it go. Not about the way he touches the curves of my cheek and chin, or the way he notices the undulating hem of my skirt, but the way the ball curves, or doesn't curve. It's mostly about that. Brett throws words at me like *slider, sinker, change up, release point,* as if they were all really important. And I throw words at him, words that seem to catch him off guard: *feelings, relationship, what we have between us.*

"How'd you get that bruise on your shoulder?" I notice a blue oval on his skin as he slides his baseball jersey over his head.

"Diving for a ball," he answers.

"Does it hurt?"

"Nope," he says as though something is obvious. "I made the catch, after all." Then I see a scar on his elbow I hadn't noticed before.

"And that scar?" I ask, pointing to it.

"Nothing," he mutters. "From a long time ago." Then he tosses his jersey to the wash basket and steps out of the room.

I want to call to him: "If the stitches on a baseball were scars, then I bet you'd talk about them." Instead I don't reply. But I know one thing for certain: I can't always stay silent like this.

2

When I talk with the other player's girlfriends at the concession stand, they complain that it's hard to find a lot in common with a ballplayer. After these months of dating Brett, I'm beginning to understand what they mean. It's the way of ballplayers, I've been thinking. Some—like Brett's buddies—never face you during a conversation, but instead stand at a forty-five-degree angle and shift their eyes toward you now and then. They seem to be popping their fists nervously in their leather gloves, though they aren't wearing gloves. I've realized that—no matter what their age—most ballplayers are just young boys underneath.

Sometimes, when he doesn't realize it, I stare at the side of Brett's face. Maybe he'll be reading the morning paper, or spooning his Wheaties from a bowl and gazing idly at the front of the orange cardboard box as he chews.

I stare because I want to know his deepest thoughts, the subtle workings inside his head. It's as though his head is some kind of complicated clock, and I want to get close enough to hear the gears moving inside it. I want to know every notch and turn in those gears.

"What are you thinking?" I ask with a lilting voice.

"Aw, nothing much," is his usual reply.

3

I've come to understand that ballplayers never move too quickly except when they're in their game and dashing toward first base or running to catch a pop-up. It's not that they're lazy; it's just that between games, they seem to conserve their energy. They're the type that tip back on their chairs and wait for life to come to them. They live game-to-game, with not much else in between. "Ballplayers need to be steady, June," Brett tells me. "You know—consistent." He nods as if agreeing with himself, and for an instant I picture him walking from the mound after an inning, careful with that odd superstition of his: not to step on the ghostly chalk of the third base line.

"Oh?" I exhale, brushing a spiral of my auburn hair from one eye.

"Yeah. They need to plan their strategy. You know, for the next game."

That's Brett, all right, I think. Steady. Maybe too steady. Though he's still young at twenty-seven, and the star pitcher on his amateur team, sometimes he seems like an old man. He'll sit in the pilled beige recliner for hours in the morning, reading the Sunday sports page, studying each stat in a box score like it was the most interesting thing in the universe. Maybe he's planning things, I tell myself. Maybe he's dreaming. Maybe green fields are unfolding behind his eyes.

Leaning my hip against the doorframe of the kitchen, I ask "Want to split this pear with me?" I hold up the overripe fruit I found, forgotten, on a back shelf of the refrigerator. It must have fallen from a tree, because there's a dark dent on one side.

"No, that's okay," he says absently, not moving, not looking at me. "Go ahead and have it."

4

During the games when I'm in the stands, Brett doesn't glance up at me when he's pitching. He never seems to look me in the eye lately, the way he stares at the batter with his opaque blue eyes when he's on the mound, or the way he peers at the catcher for the sign seconds before he rears back and fires the pitch—like a beam of light—toward home. He once told me that the look before the pitch—that glare that keeps the batter off balance—is sometimes as important as the pitch itself. When he pitches inning after inning, his eyes focus only on the thin, exact line he draws toward the plate with each pitch.

I know he wants to look at me—at least a fleeting shift of his eyes—but he's not one to do that, not even during warm-ups. And especially not between pitches, after the catcher has tossed the ball back to him and he pauses there, adjusting the bill of his cap, sliding up the sleeve of his pitching arm, staring down at the tips of his cleats as if they were so important, then pawing at the packed beige dirt of the mound as if he's trying to steady the whole earth. Maybe he thinks that if he looks at me, in my red tank top and cutoffs, leaning toward him from the top row of the wooden bleachers, he'll lose some of his concentration. Though I've asked him about it a few times, he's never really explained it.

But I think I know the reason: I think he knows that when I look at him, I see the real him, beneath the gray polyester uniform with the orange Monarchs logo on the front. I see, beneath his tanned leather skin and toned muscle, the real person, the real deep-down weak and fragile and flawed him. And that makes him nervous.

5

Fame. Lately I've noticed that ballplayers think a lot about fame. Brett's no different. He's always talking about these Hall of Fame players named Mickey or Babe or Willie or somebody, and I have to remind him that they're just people. They're just guys who happen to be skilled at hitting and catching a baseball, and nothing more.

"They're heroes," he insists. "You know—legends."

"That's what you want to be?" I question. "A baseball legend?"

When I said that, he just winced, then gave me a questioning look that said Hey, I don't have a comeback for that one.

Sometimes ballplayers don't admit it, because they play for a small-town team like the River City Monarchs, but a glimmer of fame still flickers in the backs of their brains. They still entertain the thought that they could have a couple of great seasons, be featured in the local papers, then get picked up by a minor league club. Once there, they'd show off their talents and get called up to the Majors, where they'd step on a field in a white pinstriped uniform beneath floodlights so bright they nearly burn the skin. No matter how small their life, their dreams of glory are big. Always big.

I know what they picture before warm-ups when they close their eyes and lie back on their small-town field, gloves tucked softly under their heads. They see huge stadiums. Grandstands with triple decks. A big contract from the Majors. They let those thoughts jog in circles around their brain. But each dropped ball pushes those dreams father away. So does an off-target throw. Or a swing and a miss. Or a competent but still unspectacular .250 batting average. The dream fades and gets a little smaller as each season passes, but it's still there, like a red ember glowing in the center of a circle of ashes.

Brett thinks a lot about it, I know. He worries about it, but I try to buffer him, protect him from the pain, like a padded chest guard or a catcher's mask. After a game when things don't go well for him, after a game where the opposing team scores a batch of runs off his pitching and he goes hitless, I try to buoy him up. "It's okay," I say, hoping that will help, though I can tell by the shattered look on his face it really doesn't, "It's okay. Let's talk about it." And I pull him close to me, though he resists, the muscles of his shoulders stiffening.

6

The future. Most often, that's what I try to talk to him about. The future—what's ahead. "You mean the state tourneys in August?" he asks, missing my point.

"No. Not the tournaments." I pause for a few seconds, my inhaled breath sounding like a gusting breeze on an empty field, "The future. The real future. What we have between us."

"Oh," he replies, lifting his gaze to me, blinking as if a small cloud of infield dust suddenly blew into his face. "That."

I close my eyes and wait for him to say more, but he doesn't. For the next few seconds, I feel my frustration rising, and red flashes of anger flicker behind my eyelids. Then I have to fill up the void with "Yes, that."

7

The world, I tell him. The man I love has to understand that I need the world. I need what's outside his little game. He has to know that I can't be—like he is—confined to a three-acre field, boxed in by a cyclone fence and leaning wooden dugouts and dusty chalk lines. He has to know that I can move, at any time, into the world. Into my life. He has to know that, to feel it, to understand it.

The world isn't as structured as a ball game, I say. It doesn't have nine innings, twenty-seven outs. It doesn't have a 1:00 p.m. start, and an end, a clear winner and a loser. It's not planned out, like a batting order inked on a scorecard. Still, the world is an incredible place, I tell him—mysterious, disappointing and unpredictable sometimes—but still amazing. The world is always out there, with its wild horses in canyons, its new cities of glass and ancient cities of stone, its shoeless children climbing mountains, its starkparched but oasis-dotted deserts, its palm trees bowing down to ocean shores, its orchards filled with fruit trees. I tell him that maybe the most worthwhile batting averages are calculated by what you accomplish outside the fences of a baseball field.

"Sometimes the world is like a bruised pear," I say. "It's not perfect," I explain, "but it's real, and delicious. And just waiting for you to take a bite."

As soon as I say this, he just gives me an odd, squinting look, as though his face is crisscrossed with backstop wires, and I know he doesn't quite get what I mean.

8

"So what's next?" he asks me as we stand in the kitchen of our rented apartment. I can see the tension between us pulling his usual smile away and tightening his face. He's almost late for his game, and I've just told him I'm not sure if I'm going to sit in the bleachers this time. I've just told him I might have to make a decision. That we both might have to. The tiers of cans on the cupboard shelves watch us, waiting. The Zip-Loc bags in the drawer hold their breaths. It seems like the game is tied in the late innings, and the next error, the next dropped ball, the next well-hit drive wins or loses it. The difference between a good pitch and a bad pitch is always a fraction of an inch, and I have the feeling that the next motion—wrong or right—will change the outcome forever.

"What's next, then?" he repeats. I shake my head. He should know the answer to his question.

At that moment, everything seems caught in limbo—neither of us say anything more; we're like a brown-tone sepia photo, the two of us motionless, pressed beneath a thick layer of silent glass.

9

What's next is that I break from the pause and gently lift his ball cap from his head, exposing matted brown hair that curls around his ears. He doesn't squirm, embarrassed, like he usually does.

"Want to split this pear with me?" I ask, and I hold it up by its stem. It's yellowish-green and misshapen, its skin dimpled with pores.

This time, he doesn't look away for the safety of a sports page, or his oiled leather mitt, hanging on a peg by the back door. This time he looks into my eyes as if he could get lost, or found there. And he could. I know he could.

His face slowly softens and he finally drops his guard. I can tell by the look in his eyes that the world—the whole world—is rushing into him, that he's finally understanding what I've been talking about.

"Yes," he says, his lips curving into a smile, "Definitely yes." He lifts the pear, takes a bite of it, smiles. He hands it to me, and I take a bite, too.

For the next few seconds, I sense that, in his mind, he's picturing time suddenly moving forward through the years. His winnings and losings begin to blur, and the hours of sweating practice and the batting averages and seasons of bent scorecards don't matter anymore. The tournaments and his pulled tendons and torn rotator cuffs and the limping hours of rehab and the punctured dreams fall away. Then that agonizing day passes, too: It's the day, a decade from now, when—replaced by a younger player—he's taken out of the lineup and sits on the hard pine bench, staring at the hieroglyphs on the scuffed dugout floor. That painful day and all those other moments pass.

And as for now, right now: He leans toward me as I lean toward him and our lips finally touch. I can taste that sweet pear juice on his mouth, and all his glorious baseball plans don't matter anymore.

And what replaces them is something smaller, much smaller than he ever pictured, but something more precious: It might be our first, cramped yellow two-bedroom house with aluminum siding that needs paint, a leaning wooden fence near a weed-patch garden, and a couple of kids playing catch with a Soft-strike ball in the yard. It might be laundry hanging on the line—the sun angling through the white sheets that rise, billow in the wind like the soft dreams of a cloud, then fall still again. It might be eating breakfast together, our spoons clinking against the glass bowls while we gaze through the parted curtains at that scene. It might be lifting our coffee cups slowly, in unison, and taking a sip at the same moment. It might be a pear, sliced in half, on a China plate between us. Just that small, but perfect scene. It might be that, I tell him. That might be what's next.

PART TWO:
RUNNING THROUGH
DEEP GRASS

NEWS, WEATHER AND SPORTS

I watched it on the mid-day news, but because I was only seven years old, I didn't understand what was happening. On the grainy screen of the small Motorola TV, a man folded his steel arms and blocked a dark-faced schoolgirl from entering the front door of the school. I saw police with night sticks, closing in on a group of people marching on a bridge, canisters of teargas spewing out hissing white clouds. As I left the house for my little league game, I clicked the set off, the distorted black and white images collapsing into a single dot of light in the middle of the screen.

Later that day, the fly ball rose toward me in right field. It was my first little league game, and the first ball hit at me. I had never seen a baseball rising that high, cutting the sky in half. The ball reached its highest point—a tiny, crazy, planet in orbit, and it seemed to hang in the hazy air as though it were suspended by a wire. Suddenly, the screams of the other players made the wire snap, and the ball began its sudden descent. So, I did what outfielders do. Pretending to get under it, I circled on the grass as if centering myself beneath it. I thumped my fist—like a rapid heartbeat—in the pocket of my glove. All the while, I felt panicky inside because I had no idea where the ball would come down.

In our small town, our little league field was the same field the local Negro League team, the Brownies, used for their home games. The year before, Dad took me to one of their exhibition games, telling me "You have to see them. These guys are really good."

During pre-game warm-ups, I watched the two players from the Brownies bowl the baseball on the ground to each other, while others made acrobatic behind-the-back catches. Emulating teams like the Indianapolis Clowns, the barnstorming Negro teams' reputation was to be funny, and to joke around on the field in order to entertain the all-white fans who showed up for the game. One guy did a tap dance on home plate to some scratchy piped-in Al Jolson music while the fans from our small town pointed and laughed. Another player sprinted around the bases backwards with the mascot dog—a black lab named Brownie—as the fans hooted and chuckled.

Before the game, my father and I chatted with a player named Elston. Dressed in a baggy gray flannel jersey, he leaned his slim frame on the five-foot-high fence alongside the dugout.

"How long have you played ball?" my father asked him.

"Mama claimed I played in the womb before I was born," he quipped, his big yellowish teeth showing in a grin in contrast to his deep black, almost shiny face. "When I was five, I usta bat with a broomstick. I'd hit bottle caps pitched by my brother, just for fun."

"You fellas get paid for these exhibition games, right?" Dad inquired.

"Huh," Elston laughed. "A couple bucks a game. Sometimes less." He gave us a wink. "A fella can live like royalty for that, right?" Then he added, "Really, I just play for the love of it, man. Why else?"

Then Elston nodded to me. "The boy play ball?"

"Not yet," my father answered. "But he probably will."

"Make real sure he does," Elston said. "Best game in the world."

I held up my program up to him, and he signed it with his big tawny hand, then turned and jogged out for warm-ups.

After the pre-game antics, where Elston did a little juggling act with four baseballs, he got serious and hit two home runs. One of them rose high into the night, as though gravity had no effect on it, and landed somewhere out in the cornfield beyond the center field wall. Dad had told me he was an amazing outfielder, and I saw what he meant—I watched Elston make an astounding over-the-shoulder catch in left field and throw a couple of runners out with frozen rope tosses to second base. The Brownies trounced the local all-star team—all white players from the area—winning by twelve runs. As the game ended, I saw one of the local players throw his batting helmet and bat from the dugout onto the first base line in disgust.

On the way back to the car, I asked my father "Where do players from the Brownies live, anyway?" I hadn't ever seen any of them around town.

"Down by the tracks. They work for the railroad during the day, I guess. They set up a kind of shanty town during the summer." He hesitated, then added, "I heard our city council decided to put up a fence around it."

"A fence? Why?"

"Don't know. Kind of a dividing line."

"Dividing line? For what?"

Dad thought for a few seconds. "To separate our town from theirs, I guess."

I looked down at the program clutched in my hand and studied Elston's scrawled autograph. "Think Elston will make it to the Major Leagues?"

Dad put the Plymouth in first gear and pulled the car from the parking lot, gravel making a low popping sound beneath the tires. "I'm not sure about that." He adjusted the mirror.

"Why not?" I questioned. "You said he was a great hitter. Better than all the guys on our town team. Right?"

"Well, um, yeah," he replied tentatively, his eyes glancing left and right at the upcoming intersection. Some inattentive driver had bumped into the stop sign, and it leaned slightly to one side. "He's got the skills. But still, it'd be a hard road for him."

"But why?" I quizzed. To me, Elston seemed like he'd be a star Major Leaguer. At that age, I knew nothing about the sting of prejudice against black ballplayers like Jackie Robinson or Hank Aaron. At some restaurants, after the black ballplayers ate there, the manager would collect their plates and smash them in the back room. I never heard about Whites Only signs at drinking fountains, about explosions erupting in black Baptist churches. Our central Iowa's radio station focused mainly on the grain report and the new petunia garden the Ladies Auxiliary planted on the courthouse square, the chances of rain in the next growing season, and the scores from last week's Men's Bowling League at the VFW.

News, weather, sports. Always in that same order, as if those were the only three things in the world.

My father didn't answer as we passed Ned's Hardware with its cracked picture window and Nick's Barber Shop with the candy cane-striped pole that rotated, spiraling endlessly upward toward the blue awning. I heard a tick tick tick of the turn signal inside the cloth interior of the car as Dad approached the turn onto Main.

But I couldn't let the subject drop. "Tell me, Dad. Why can't he join the Majors? Why can't he be on the Yankees or the Dodgers?" I insisted. "You said he was great, didn't you?"

When we paused at the town's one stop light, Dad's hands clenched and unclenched the amber steering wheel. "He is," he finally said, focusing on the red light. "He is talented. But colored players, I mean… they have to be more than great to make it in the big leagues." Then he added, with a sigh, "They're not even allowed at the café in town." He pinched his lips together so they almost disappeared. The light glared through the windshield a few more seconds, giving his face a pink tinge. Then he added, "It's kind of the way of things, I guess."

My face melted into a frown. All I could do was picture Elston, loping around the bases after he hit that ball a mile over the left field fence. I pictured that white baseball, rolling all the way toward the bank of the slate gray river that slid past the edge of town.

Dad and I continued the drive through town, riding beneath the looming shadow of the tin grain elevator and then passing the Co-op and the ten-foot high sculpture of an ear of corn, placed there by the Chamber of Commerce. I couldn't stop looking at it, poised there—deaf and silent and made of concrete.

Before my first little league game, the team captain—a big kid two years older than me—had griped "Outfielder? You don't look like an outfielder. Too skinny. Too short. Too weird."

Not having enough players, he put me in anyway, and when our team took the field for the first time that humid summer afternoon, I ran out to right field at full speed, coughing after I inhaled a couple of gnats that spiraled above the grass. Pretending to know where to stand, I spun around and faced the infield. I poised there, nervously grinding my fist in my glove, chewing hard on two sticks of spearmint gum. Between pitches, I leaned forward, placing my hands on my knees like I saw players do during the sports report on the TV. I stood there beneath the intense, staring sun, waiting to become an outfielder. I knew I had to prove to the team captain that I'd transformed from an ordinary, weak kid pedaling a small Schwinn bicycle to a real baseball player. And for a few seconds, I started to believe it.

But my belief vanished when a tall, muscular twelve-year-old stepped to the plate with the bases loaded. He swung at the first pitch and the baseball rocketed from his bat. It was launched right at me. During those few stretched-out seconds it climbed the air until it nearly disappeared—a tiny black hole in the dome of the sky.

For an instant, somewhere in the back of my mind, I might have had a fleeting image of Elston during the games my father and I had watched him play. I might have pictured Elston—leaping high in the air, high enough to catch a ball destined to clear the left field fence. As he roamed the outfield, it seemed like there were no fences for him. Though I knew my world and my barriers were just little ones, in the back of my mind, I might have been thinking, *If he can do it, then so can I.*

The fly ball reached its height and then began to streak downward, a meteor breaking the surface of the atmosphere. As it did, the swirling wind gusted toward me, carrying with it voices—not just the encouraging shouts of my teammates but the catcalls and jeers of the other team, too. The words clashed together. Drop it! Catch it! Drop it! Catch it! I tipped my face toward the sky, popped my fist in the glove confidently.

Then the voices all went silent, and I heard the ball land at least thirty feet behind me.

At that moment, the sound of the five-ounce baseball striking the ground was the loudest sound I'd ever heard. It was a dull sound, a muffled thump, yet it was deafening in my ears and resonated inside my skull, as if someone had dropped a dream to the sidewalk. As if someone had just knocked the wind out of the earth a little.

I don't remember exactly what happened after that. I probably dashed frantically to pick the ball up as my teammates groaned and yelled "Awwww, Jeeze!" and "Come on!" and the big kid's teammates cheered him while he rounded the bases and all four runs scored. I probably threw a wild, off-target, rainbow-shaped throw back toward the second baseman, who had to run halfway into the outfield to retrieve the ball on first or second bounce.

What I did know was that I misjudged that ball, and afterwards I stood there for the rest of the inning, wiping the sweat from my forehead, the magnified afternoon heat seeming to press a weight on my shoulders. A few excuses sprinted through my head. I wanted to tell my teammates it was the fault of the wind. Or gnats got in my eyes and made them water. Or the ball—hit so hard—was curving away from me. But I knew they wouldn't believe any of those things.

After the inning was over, I began a slow trot toward the bench, dreading, like an oncoming storm, the way my teammates would chide me and shake their heads. I feared that our team captain—who stood there, frowning with his arms crossed—would bench me. I braced myself for the humiliation.

But then something eased my anxiety. As I shuffled hesitantly across the infield, I noticed someone by the side of the field.

It was Elston. He'd been watching the game.

Already suited up in his Brownies jersey for his evening game, he leaned his lanky body on the cyclone fence beyond the first base line. I knew that, unlike me, he could leap right over that fence if he wanted to. He didn't say anything as I passed him, just gave me a quick nod and a fleeting tight-lipped half-smile.

I paused, nodded back, then turned to face the dugout while, above all of us, the sun shrunk to a single pale dot in the middle of the grainy sky.

EL RELAMPAGO

He'll tell you his name is Rivera, and he has begun to believe that his feet have wings.

He'll tell you his name is Rivera, and he lives just a mile down the road from Chichén Itza, the famous Maya ruin, and he plays baseball in the Mexican winter league.

But more than anything, he wants to play in the American Major Leagues. His name is Rivera—a small, lithe man who fields well but does not have great batting power, so he's learned to develop his one talent, and his talent, he will tell you, is his speed. His speed. *Velocidad.* When he runs the base paths, he thinks of himself as the speed of sound, speed of light, speed of time. He's come to be known as the best base stealer in Mexican baseball. *El Relampago*, his teammates call him. Lightning. "You could be a legend in the American Big Leagues," his teammate Luis once said to him, "if they'd only give you a chance." Though he shrugs, he knows how much he wants to run after that chance, knows he could catch up to it, no matter how far out of reach it might be, knows he would dive for it the same way he leaps head-first into second base when he hears the ball hissing toward the glove, his outstretched fingertips reaching it in plenty of time to fall in love with the worn canvas bag.

Summer evenings, with the baby asleep, his wife might sit in the doorway and gaze at the road toward Merida, watching the last bus filled with tourists roar past, a wake of blue exhaust rising. And Rivera might lie for a few minutes in a hammock tied between two trees beside his small thatched-roofed house and gaze at his wife and child their dark brown beauty framed by the crooked doorway. As the chickens run beneath him in a squawk of feathers, and the scruffy dogs chase their tails by the shed, he thinks about the Major Leagues: the shiny helmets, the bats which are not chipped, their veneer smooth on the barrels, the cleats with white shoe laces—not the dust-brown laces on the scuffed cleats he wears when he plays for his Yucatan team. For most men in the countryside, this time after dinner is a time of rest, a time to relax from a long day of work, to think of sleep. But this evening, after a few minutes in the hammock, Rivera swings his feet to the hard-packed ground, strolls over, kisses his wife on the cheek, and turns from her.

"Corriendo?" Jacinta asks, as she always does. "Running?"

"Si," he replies, and as he hears her voice behind him call "Always running," he is already cutting a diagonal across the yard, leaping over the rusted oil drums in the ditch and jogging down the road toward Chichén Itzá. As he runs the mile down the dirt road from his house, the famous Maya Pyramids begin to rise up from the jungle growth. He sees them ahead—massive ruins, some of them vine-draped, lifting their stone shoulders into the steamy air, silhouetted against the rolling gray and white clouds in the distance. All but a few of the tourists, with their crisscross of camera straps, have left on the busses to Merida or Cancun, and, near dusk, he is practically alone at the ruins. He lopes to the Great Ball Court alongside the pyramid and pauses to stare at the carvings in the stone. The stone hoop is thirty feet above the court on the wall. To make a score, the players had to bounce the ball through that hoop without using their hands. They had to be fast, and agile, and strong. "The winners took all," he says each day to the tourists, "and the losers were sacrificed." Rivera stares at the stone carvings where the winners, lifting triumphant swords to the sky, hold the losers' heads by their hair.

Summer afternoons, Rivera works part-time as a tourist guide, leading Americans from their American Express busses through the ruins of a great culture. "I am called Rivera," he says at the beginning of the tour and also at the end, "I am your guide, and I also play base-ball, or, as we call it, *beisbol*." He tells all the stories he's heard about Chichén, the legends and half-truths spoken by the elders and Maya ancestors, and then he tells them the experts' explanations which he's studied in books at the University of Mexico. He describes Quetzal-cóatl, the Feathered Serpent, the legendary god of Aztec and Toltec cultures, whose image is carved throughout the park, including in El Castillo, the largest pyramid. "At the solstice at dawn," he tells them, "the image of the snake appears as a shadow crawling down the corner of the pyramid." He points to the carved head. "And the shadow attaches perfectly to the carved serpent's head at the base. It is complete symmetry, complete beauty." While he speaks, the tourists gaze in wonder beyond him at the grand limestone edifices.

He explains how the pyramids were built from the ground up. Centuries ago, the first primitive settlers built crude shrines in this area, and each new generation added their shrines and temples to the base. "Here," he narrates with his strong Mexican accent, "the buildings are as unique as any in the world. You find culture upon culture. Civilization upon civilization." As he scans the puffy faces of the American tourists, he thinks how there is so much they don't know. *Life is quick, it's easy and convenient in the Estados Unidos, he thinks. There is so little history. Two hundred years, and before that, nothing. A blink of an eye.*

"What did they worship?" a tourist occasionally asks. This week, it was a broad man, his breasts bulging beneath his powder blue Ralph Lauren Polo knit shirt.

"The same things we all do," he replies. "The sun, the moon. The rain god. The god of growing. The Jaguar, for its fleetness of foot."

When he says this, the tourists always give him a puzzled look. Then they might turn away, maybe snap a photo of their tour bus, a photo which they'll look at later to see that it's over-exposed, the red and blue enamel faded.

Early summer mornings, before the tourist busses arrive, Rivera practices baserunning on the jungle-surrounded ball field at the edge of the little village close to his house. He stands a few feet off first base—a warped square of tin cut from a drum—and imagines a pitcher, trying to pick him off. He practices it over and over: the waiting. *You must be in complete balance, he thinks. Equilibrio. If you're caught leaning, you're dead.* Then, the instant the imaginary pitcher makes the slightest move toward home, Rivera lunges, the piston of his left leg driving him into motion. He digs toward second, digs, head down, his legs a blur, clumps of orange clay flipping from his cleats and thumping against his back, and he's there. Later, he might practice his evasive slide, a quick sweeping motion along the outside of the bag as he grabs it with his left hand. In this way, he builds one skill upon another skill. He knows they all add up. When they all work together in a game, he's fluid, he's pure grace as he dashes down the baseline. No one could throw him out, no one. He must believe this. He is Rivera Ligero, and he could be the fastest man in baseball. Speed, anyone would call him if they saw him run. El *Rapido*. He could outrun the strong wind and drag it by the hair.

When he looks up, he's surprised to see the small children from the village who have gathered along the first base line to watch, their broad brown Maya faces smiling in awe. As he dashes from first to second, they laugh and try to run along with him, though they can never catch him. "Why do you run?" one small boy, barefoot and dressed in torn khaki shorts, asks and Rivera jogs back to first base.

"Why do you see though your eyes?" Rivera responds.

For a moment, there's a confused look in their high cheek-boned faces; then they giggle and smile. After the kids tire of chasing him and walk away to other games, he runs wind-sprints on the field. He pushes himself until his heart beats so hard it feels as though it might burst from the narrow cage of his ribs. He runs, runs some mornings until his lungs draw in the whole smooth Mexican sky.

Rivera leans toward the day when he will play in the professional leagues. He longs for it, and often envisions himself on a real team in Texas or Arizona, a place to hang your uniform besides a peg on the wall of the rusted tin and bamboo stand used for his home team's dugout. Rivera sometimes thinks he would sacrifice anything to make it to the American Major Leagues. He knows that if he does not eventually make it with a team—even a single-A team in the States, he will die a little inside. He will die a little, as if a part of himself were cut out from his center and tossed to the sun-beaten limestone to dry and wither.

Summer mornings and afternoons, he shepherds the tourists through the remains of an extinct city. The broad backs of the tourists' khaki shirts are always dark with sweat as, puffing, they sidestep through the maze of excavated buildings and walls of Chichén Itzá. "Take your time," he tells them. "Slow down. *Mira. Look.*" He describes the Temple of the Jaguar, telling the tourists that the Maya worshipped the Jaguar for its quickness, its agility, its beauty. The Maya built many shrines for the Jaguar, and they sculpted Jaguar effigies in valuable stone, but none so magnificent as the stone Jaguar found hidden inside the temple in the great pyramid at Chichén Itzá.

In the Mexican winter league, Rivera's team from the Yucatán, the *Jaguars,* plays teams like the *Tomateros* and the *Yanquis* on fields with hard reddish dirt infields, the tropical grass growing in raised clumps in the outfield. Once a large green iguana had to be removed from center field, its tail flopping. In the towns further north, like Mexicali, the spikes of cactus rise just beyond the outfield fences, and snakes curl in wedges of sun beneath the bleachers. Before the games he sits on the bench with his friends, Manny and Antonio and Luis. Rivera knows their longing. They talk of playing American baseball all the time, of contracts and staying in carpeted hotel rooms with large, clean showers and big, flat-screen television sets, of getting rich with the New York Yankees. They dream of riding in shiny cars, wearing gold chains, and eating dinners in restaurants with cloth tablecloths and glistening silverware.

But Rivera's dreams of the major leagues are not about the money, like his teammates. His dream is a simple one: He just wants to feel the soul of a Major League field rise up through his legs as he leads off base for the first time. He hasn't thought about it beyond that simple moment: just being there, in a huge, clean stadium, to get the chance to lead off first base. And though he would look appear casual, all his muscles would be alert and balanced.

Rivera can't help but notice the hope in his teammates' brown eyes. It's the same hope he saw in the small girls' eyes as they sold trinkets—cloth pouches and brightly-colored woven bracelets—on the streets of Tijuana. When he visited there once, a small, smudged-faced girl held the trinkets out to tourists, and said, in English, "Three for a dolla? Three for a dolla?" while the tourists brushed past her without looking. But Rivera looked into her eyes as she turned toward him, and he saw the depth of pain in those brown liquid pools. He saw his whole country in her eyes. He wondered how long it would take to leave her poverty behind. Probably her whole lifetime. He pulled out a 200-peso bill and bought some brightly-colored bracelets to take back to his wife. He told the girl to keep the extra pesos, and she gave him a quizzical half-smile.

Rivera set a record for base stealing last season; sometimes, before the catchers even looked up and realized it, he was standing on second base. *"El Jaguar,"* his teammates call him with a laugh. "You can dash around all the bases in eleven or twelve seconds, amigo," says Luis, the portly catcher. "Too fast for your own good, that's what you are."

Between innings, they sit on the bench and snack on hand-slapped tortillas, drink papaya juice or horchata. After the games, Rivera and his teammates often buy helado or sopapillas from the concession stand, the honey dripping on their palms like yellow pine tar. Or, after a home game, they might stop for *Dos Equis* or tequila at the local cantina. Once, when Rivera was looking the other way, a small goat ambled through the open adobe doorway and drank from his glass of beer at the low wooden table. When Rivera turned back to his glass, the goat bolted out the door, and they all laughed until tears rolled down their cheeks. "Why didn't you chase him, amigo?" Luis asked after a couple of cervezas. "You are too fast for words," Luis joked. He took a gulp of *Negra Modelo*, laughed like some squawking jungle bird, and slapped Rivera on the back. "You could outrun time, amigo. The rest of us grow old, but not little Rivera. You're so fast you could run and leave yourself behind."

The Maya culture fell into ruin, and no one really knows why, Rivera explains to the tourists. "The Maya were amazing," he says. *Asombroso*. He tells them they invented the zero in mathematics, they devised an accurate calendar, developed sophisticated festivals and sports. They had all the riches of wealth and the arts. A huge cultural city with five hundred thousand people existed right where you stand, he tells them, and then *suddenly*, it was gone. Time passes so quickly, and the civilization was gone. Now, all that is left is a few ruins above ground and its soul, below the ground. A mystery. No one knows the secret. "Was it war?" he asks. As he pauses a moment, pacing his delivery, as confused looks cross the faces of the tourists. "Were they forced out by an inferior, warring tribe? Was it famine? Was it a long drought? Was it the sacrifice of the strongest young males, their hearts ripped out for all to see?" He pauses for five seconds, timing it just right. No one," he says slowly, and with drama, "no one knows for certain."

Rivera leads off third base, the large stadium surrounding him filled with cheering fans. When he dashes toward home, the distance between third and home seems to lengthen as he runs, as if someone was pulling the earth out from under him. He runs and runs and runs, panting, but he doesn't seem to get any closer. It's then that he wakes from the dream, sweating in his small bamboo house with the thatched roof. It's then that he wakes up and touches his numb legs, runs his fingernails along the shin bones to make sure they're still there.

"Rivera?" his wife's soft, half-sleeping voice whispers. His thrashing has wakened her. "What is it, Rivera? *El sueño de correr?* The dream of running?"

He nods.

"Running," she says, exasperated. "Always running. Running when you're awake, running when you sleep. What will it take to slow you down, Rivera Ligero? What will it take to catch you?"

"No one will catch me," he says.

"Not even me?" she asks, the disappointment weighing down her voice.

"*Si,*" he says, laughing, "Maybe you. Maybe just you."

"Sometimes," she sighs, "sometimes I'm afraid you'd give up anything to get to the Major Leagues," she says. "Sometimes I think you will run away and leave me behind."

Without another word, he turns toward her and embraces her. He inhales her fragrant scent of hyacinths and jungle flowers. He kisses her on the lips and her lips push back at him; the kiss tastes of sweet, ripe papaya, and soft, warm clay. "*Jamas sueñas de mi?*" she whispers. "Am I ever your dream?"

"*Si,*" he answers, "*Siempre.* Always."

They make love in the humid darkness. The flowing curves of her tawny skin rise and fall beneath the touch of his fingertips. Afterwards, panting, they stare into the deep brown of each other's eyes, and nothing needs to be said. There are no words to translate what they're feeling.

The next morning, at Chichén Itzá, Rivera ushers the tourists toward the Sacred Cenote, where, legend has it, human sacrifices took place. The cenote is a huge well, a hundred feet in diameter, and two hundred feet to the dark green, algae-coated water below. The walls are slick limestone.

"A mysterious place, full of questions," he says. He explains that beneath its murky waters, explorers have found some answers: excavators found gold jewelry, precious stones and human bones. It is thought that the sacrificial victims were drugged and then thrown into the Sacred Cenote, where, because it was impossible to climb out, they drowned. The sacrifices appeased the Rain God in times of drought, he explains to the tour group; it assured rain and a fertile planting season. "The clay is slippery near the lip of the cenote," he warns, "so do not venture too close, *amigos.*"

As Rivera's one-hour tour nears its end, he has to slow down for the out-of-shape tourists, who begin to puff and gasp for breath. He slows down for them, and then gazes at the great pyramid and thinks about the levels upon levels of the stairs.

"Anybody ever climb that big ol' thing?" an overweight man in a Georgia Bulldogs t-shirt once asked him during a tour.

"Sí," Rivera answered. "I do."

The tourists who visit Chichén Itzá love Rivera's tour, his banter and jokes, his quick, encompassing smile. "Brilliant," one couple remarks at the conclusion of the tour. "You should work as a guide full-time. You should make this your career."

"No, no," he replies modestly. "It is only a seasonal job. My dream is to play American baseball. Then he pushes himself to add, "Some call me *El Relampago*, the fastest player in Mexico."

They nod and give him polite smiles and snap shots of him with their cell phones before they board the bus back to Mérida or Cancún to their luxury all-inclusive hotels and their flights back to New Jersey or Michigan or Ohio.

Some nights Rivera dreams of storm clouds sliding quickly overhead, and the rain falling. The clay beneath his bare feet turns quickly to mud and he can feel himself slipping. He tries to pivot on his heel, tries to turn and climb away from the edge, but the more his legs try to move, the more he's slipping backwards into it. In the dream, he's not quick enough—everything moves in slow motion, as if he's a stone statue trying to break out of its mold, and he hates that feeling. He's weighted down with gold necklaces and bracelets, and a mask of gold hinders his vision. Then, suddenly, he's falling, falling head over heels in the humid air, the pale limestone walls of the cenote rushing past him. He's falling, and as he strikes the water, he wakes and sits up in bed, his forehead damp and sweating, his heart throbbing in his chest like a bird caught in a cage too small. His wife's hands rush to him, touching his sweating forehead, calming him.

"*Corriendo?*" she asks. "*Estabas corriendo?* Don't run away from me, or from your young daughter. I love you, Rivera."

This evening, after dinner, he kissed Jacinta as she sat on the doorstep, and began his run toward Chichén Itzá just before dusk.

When he arrives at the grounds, the park is closed, and he's alone, except for a few local children playing kick ball. One boy, recognizing him from the time he practiced on the local field, waves. Rivera waves back, then slides under the security fence and jogs up the great pyramid, step by step, working his legs. The stone stairs are high, and he must pull his knees up to reach each step, but it can be done. At the top, he pauses, panting for breath, and looks across the ruins to the steamy, vine-choked jungle, so green, and so impassable. He hears, below, the sound of the children laughing as they bounce the ball rhythmically off the base of the pyramid with a hollow thumping sound, a heartbeat.

He watches the white cumulus clouds billowing up in the distance, and at that moment, he wonders if he could ever leave this place, this land with its rich, tangled green beauty, its warm stars slowly shifting in the night sky above the thatched roofs. He wonders if what Luis says is true—maybe he's too fast for his own good, the way he yearns so much lately for America and the Major Leagues.

He ponders the mysteries of the Aztec, the Toltec, the Maya, and wonders if maybe he could be the one to figure out the secret of why they disappeared. Maybe he knows their secret right now, without even studying. *They ran*. Maybe they had visions of a better life, and they picked up and ran to find it.

Perhaps they searched for better crops, better land. Perhaps they ran from the love the land gave them. Perhaps they were just just too full of their own riches, their own visions. They ran, and by the time they got where they thought they wanted to be, they turned around, and it was too late to go back to where they came from. They had sacrificed everything. They ran so far they got themselves lost, and one by one, they disappeared in the jungle and perished.

He finds himself standing in front of the Tabernacle of the Jaguar inside the pyramid. He's climbed the dank, narrow steps inside El Castillo to the top of the dimly-lit interior chamber. The carved Jaguar is painted red, and its mouth is open in a mid-roar. Its back is flat like a small altar or throne, with a circle of offerings in its center. Rivera stares into the jaguar's jade-green eyes for a few moments as if they will tell him the secret. But the jaguar, its quickness held motionless by solid stone, reveals nothing.

Outside the pyramid again, Rivera gazes out over the landscape, watches the spears of yellow lightning stab into the horizon from the rolling thunderhead clouds. The children are gone, but he thinks he sees someone standing below, far across the wide courtyard, near the ball court. The person looks a lot like Jacinta. Jacinta, the one who never runs from him, the one who loves him. She's standing there, waiting for him. She cups her hands as if to call to him: *Who do you love, Rivera Ligero?* But he can't hear the words because of the tumbling roar of thunder. He pauses there on the top, and he knows she's waiting for him to walk down to toward her.

Rivera looks around to see that he's in a Major League stadium where the stairways to the upper deck are like the high steps that lead up a pyramid. He's been here so many times before in his dreams—in San Diego or Texas or Boston—that he's not sure if this one is real, or just another vision. But the smooth cream jersey squeezing his skin makes him think that it's real. So do the new white shoelaces on his shiny shoes, the touch of the groomed infield beneath his shiny cleats, the clean canvas corner of first base that caresses his toe.

He sees Jacinta's face and his young child's face in the front row in the grandstands. Both of them look into his eyes. *Love*, he thinks, *love is stronger than speed, than time.* He understands this finally, feels it all the way down and into his bones. *Love, my destination.*

As Rivera leads off the base, his heart is already beating rapidly, yet he's poised and standing still. He sets his eyes intently on the pitcher and waits. Waits for that first infinitesimal move toward the plate. When the pitcher begins his motion, time seems to slow, to pause a few seconds. Inside that moment, though it feels a little like his legs are made of stone, Rivera takes his first step.

THE KEYS

The key, he tells himself, is to just keep going.

The key is to focus on the colors that are just up ahead.

Right now, he's aiming his used Volkswagen van with the pop-up top along Florida's Route One, the highway that leads to the southernmost tip of America, where, he's heard, it comes to a dead end at Key West. Right now, he's checking the gas in his tank, and assumes he can make it at least to one of those lower keys—Kudjoe Key or somewhere—where he'll pull into a campground or maybe a park and sleep there. The lower keys are only four hours away, he knows, as he accelerates from a stoplight south of Miami. He'll get there soon, if he just keeps going.

Back in Wisconsin, in a town called North Freedom, he dyed his hair blonde before he took off on this trip. Colors are important, he tells himself, and he didn't want that brown hair anymore. It looked too dull when he stared into the mirror. And then there were those first few streaks of gray on his temples. He hated those streaks.

Colors are important, and maybe all that matter now: his blondish hair, his white cargo shorts, his yellow knit shirt. He pictures more colors that he'll see in a few miles: the green of the swaying palm trees, their leaves rustling like they're trying to tell each other something. That green, and beyond it, the blueness. The deep aqua blue of the ocean. These are the things that matter. He keeps his thoughts tight, focused on those colors.

He heard there's a place along The Keys—a narrow strip of land— where you can see the ocean on each side. The Gulf of Mexico, the Atlantic, separated by one thin concrete strand.

He wants to find that place.

If he does, he'll pull his van over, maybe crack a can of beer, and celebrate. He'll toast the highway—a highway that's become an island, paralleled on both sides by two oceans.

He thought about both sides before he left. He thought about his life at home and his life on the road. And he decided that his life should be in motion. Keep going—that was his new motto. Don't stop. Don't look back. A town named North Freedom was a misnomer; it was anything but free. Just look ahead in the wavering heat, toward the water mirage on the road.It evaporates just as you approach it, and then reappears another hundred yards down the highway. That's what you have to chase, he tells himself. That's what you have to follow. That's what keeps you moving.

Since he and his wife broke up, he's just kept moving. That was his new motto. *A body in motion stays in motion until something stops it, right?* he thinks. He learned that in physics class, back in high school. A thousand years ago. It was the law of inertia, and he'd follow that rule.

He was freestyling now, and liking it. Not a northern Midwest boy, lost in the woods. He was a surfer, a beachcomber searching for unique shells, a carefree man who braided palm fronds into necklaces for a living. No one to tell him where to turn or not turn. No umpires, calling him out, like on the last game he played for his hometown amateur team when he tried to leg it toward home from first on a double.

He was on his own. That was the key. He was heading south to escape the encroaching layers of cold. He was migrating, stopping in towns along the way, drinking a *Special Export or Key West Sunset Ale,* talking to strangers on the bar stools next to him. In Lauderdale, at the Elbo Room, when the man next to him—a paunchy guy in his 40s—asked where he was headed, he said "To the Keys. Just the Keys, that's all." He felt like that was all he needed to say. He told the man that his name was Lance, even though that wasn't his name. Lance just sounded right. Lance would be a casual guy with a stash of weed in his pocket.

"Which key?" the guy asked. He seemed knowledgeable, like a boat captain, maybe, with his Hemingway beard and a faded ball cap frayed around the rim.

"Any one'll do," he replied. Then he recited a few that he'd memorized. "There's Plantation Key, Deer Key, Grassy Key, Fiesta Key, Islamorada…" He paused there, knowing that he could keep going with the list, but it might bore the man, so he stopped. Then he added "There's sixty or seventy of them to choose from. Hundreds more off shore, even. People build houses out there on the small ones, go back and forth to the mainland by boat."

"So, you a fisherman, then?" the man inquired.

"Yeah. Fishing for life, that is," he said with a laugh, causing the man's face to scrunch into a puzzled stare.

Now, as he drives on a bridge at the edge of Windley Key, just beyond Key Largo, the memory burns in his head again. He sees he and his wife as they argued and argued that evening in June after she told him about how she felt. Or how she *didn't* feel, to be more exact.

"I just don't know about us," she said, blindsiding him that day when he came home from work. "There are other things…" she said.

"Like what?" he asked.

"Just, you know… things."

"Can you be any more vague?" he demanded.

She didn't reply for a few seconds, then finally said "I hate the color of our walls. There. Is that specific enough for you?"

He just stared at her, dumfounded. Their walls were painted an unobtrusive pale white.

As the fight began to escalate, he shouted at her, and she shouted back, their voices practically cracking the plaster ceiling of the room. He pictures her again, before she turned from the room and walked out, throwing a China plate down hard on the kitchen floor, the pieces skittering to the four corners of the room. Then she packed some things and walked out the door, leaving him standing there, still in the kitchen, hands in the pockets of his dress slacks. She'd walked out on him twice before, but she always came back. But this time, the third time, she was gone for good.

Later, in the middle of the night, in the diffused light of the kitchen, he found himself sweeping up some of the pieces of the China plate. He pushed the broom into each corner, numbly dragging the glass fragments into a dustpan. Nothing could make that plate whole again. He knew that. As he got down on hands and knees and grasped a jagged piece under the kitchen table, he cut himself, stared at the small stream of blood spiraling around and around his index finger.

One evening, a few weeks later, he heard from her again. A text on his phone, a damn black and white text, telling him she was sorry, but a lot had changed. Asking him to drop off or mail her clothes and things to her at her new address in a nearby town, if he could. She tried to make it all sound so casual, with a few emojis thrown in. There was another man in her life. She'd been seeing him a while, actually. She was in love, she wrote.

In love. Those two words stung him the most. Those two words burned themselves into the screen of his cell phone, seeming to make the screen slowly melt. He rushed into his back yard and threw the phone, hard, into the thick grove of trees. He heard it clunk against something out there in the darkness.

The next day, he left town. He took off before his next scheduled amateur baseball game—and end-of-the-season playoff game where he would have been starting in center field. Just up and left that day, without telling any of his teammates that he'd played with for years. Up and left, leaving a blank square, a hole on the roster sheet where his name used to be. As he drove past the city limits, he pictured the house he left behind, the bedroom, his shape, a sagging dent on the bed where he used to lie next to her. The house could sink into the ground, he thought. It could be torn to pieces by a tornado, a hurricane, a flood. For all he cared, it could burn until it was a flat pile of goddamn ashes.

But all that was months ago, when he started this journey, the compass needle pointing him south.

The key, he thinks now, is to not think about any of that. He clutches the steering wheel, checks the gas gauge, the thin red tongue of the needle still halfway between F and E. The key is to remember the brightness of the colors: his blonde hair, those baggy white shorts he's wearing, the yellow knit shirt he picked up new, the tag still attached to it, at a Salvation Army store. He focuses on the landscape as he drives—the turquoise waters, the verdant palms, the deep azure of the clear sky that seems to push itself into forever.

What's important, he tells himself, is to know where you're going and not know where you're going at the same time.

The key is to press the accelerator, to leave your doubts behind you like those dull gray coral rocks on the shoulder of the road.

No tears, he tells himself. There should never be tears. No thoughts about her, in love.

The key is to drive until the static hiss on the radio tells you how far you are from everything.

He's leaving the northland behind, with its frozen winter ball fields. It's December, and in the small town in Wisconsin, where he's from, the infield is a frozen pond. Beneath layers of snow, home plate is like a brittle face iced over.

But there's no ice here in winter, no wind chill warnings: just wavering heat rising from the soft tar on the road ahead. No travel advisories about blowing and drifting snow warning you to stay off the roads. Here, it's just eighty degrees and sunny. He'll get there, eventually, to the southernmost point of the U.S.—Key West. He'll get there, eventually, he tells himself— to that town where, he's heard, barefoot locals ride beat-up bikes and live in Bahamian-style houses and sell hats made of palm fronds. They play saxophones on the street corner next to their dogs that they've dressed up with tinsel and sunglasses. They play guitar on Mallory Square at sunset, the open mouth of the black guitar case waiting for occasional tips.

He'll get there and stand at that place he's dreamed about. The edge of America.

He'll tell people his name is Chad, or Shane, even though those are not his name. He'll curl his fingers into the bars of the fence along that southernmost shore and stare, with awe, at the choppy surface, the place where the waters of the Gulf meet the Atlantic. He won't let the salty ocean breeze make his eyes water. He'll just stare far off, beyond the waves; out there lies Cuba, and more islands in the Caribbean. Hundreds of them. Places where you could forget your name.

"So, you staying on the Keys?" a young man asks. The guy's in his early twenties, tanned and buffed, wearing an expensive burgundy and violet Tommy Bahama shirt and sitting on a bar stool next to his young wife. The three of them have been chatting a few minutes. Small talk. They're sitting in one of those lower Keys beach bars, with the sand floor where it's hard to tell if the pelicans perched on posts are real ones or statues. It's a place called Coco's Bar and Grill, or The Lorelei, or Snook's Hideaway, or maybe none of those.

"Anyplace I can find," he replies illusively, "or any place that finds *me*. I'll camp at a roadside, maybe. Or on a beach." Then he names a few destinations, to show he knows what he's doing: *Conch Key, Little Torch Key, Sugarloaf Key. Crawl Key, even.* All those keys he's never visited, though their colors were already vivid inside his head. "My favorite is Summerland Key," he bluffs, because he's never been there. "I like the idea of any place called *summer land.*"

"Rad," the guy replies. "We're renting a condo in the Truman Annex near Duval Street. In Key West." Before he leaves, the man stands from his bar stool, pulls his wife close to him, and, handing over his iPhone, asks, "Hey, can you take our pic? We're on our honeymoon. We'd do a selfie, but we want a full-length one."

"Sure." He nods to the beaming couple—the woman's adoring gaze, her diamond ring glistening as she lifts her hand to steady her fashionable floppy straw hat. For a second, he can't help but picture them in their condo bed, making love. Then he centers them on the screen of the cell phone.

Behind them, over the water edged by mangroves, a couple of seagulls, buoyed on the warm air, pause like parentheses. Later, he knows, the sun will set on that horizon, surprising the sky with red and pink spokes, sharp as daggers.

"Thanks, man," the guy exhales, giving him a high five. "What's your name, anyway?"

"Tab," he replies, with the first hip name he can think of. He wants to sound free. Unique. Like a surfer, maybe.

The guy checks the picture, grins, then holds the phone to his wife. "We're posting this one on Instagram, babe."

As he gives the couple a wan smile, he pictures his own wife. They were married twelve years ago, when they were both twenty-two; they exchanged their vows in a small church. *Vows*, he thinks now. *Vows are lies.* She might as well have reared back and tossed her wedding ring into the ocean. She might as well have just thrown it into the oncoming waves, where it would be quickly covered with silt. No one could never retrieve it, not by scooping handfuls of sand with their palms, or pacing in the shallows with a metal detector. No mystic psychic could locate it. It was gone, washed away, inhaled by the hourglass sands. Just like the love he thought they shared.

His mind skips to the afternoon he threw that ball from center. He threw it as hard as he could to get the runner out at home. It was his last play on the ball team, his last few moments on the field before he left town. His throw—which felt like bee stings on the inside of his arm—was a little too late and slightly off line; the runner slid under the tag and the umpire called him safe. Afterwards, a beige cloud of dust drifted from the batters' box to the bleachers behind home plate.

Today he has the impulse to throw his own wedding ring into the ocean at a wayside, but he knows he might need to pawn it for some extra gas money. He keeps the gold band in the van's ash tray for the time being, closing the tin lid on its dull gleam.

The key is to keep things where they belonged—the ring in the ash tray. The memories—keep them back there, where they belong. Don't let them catch up to you. Outrace them. Outrace them. Leave the broken ice, the clouds of dust behind.

The van's worn tires clunk over a torn-up stretch of asphalt, bringing him back. Then the road smooths itself out to fresh tar, and the tires sing their low-pitched tune again. Behind him, the narrow highway stretches all the way to the mainland, and ahead, to the horizon. *Highway and horizon*, he thinks. *Tires and pavement:* like the equinox, everything seems pretty much aligned. And there he was, somewhere in the middle, right there, sort of caught between everything, but still free. He cranks up the volume on the a.m. radio, set on a '90s channel.

The next thing he knows, a small red light blinks out of the center of his rearview mirror. The light grows in size, flashing at him. The rising and falling sound of a siren burns his ears. He glances at the speedometer and realizes he's going over eighty.

"Damn!" he spits as he slows and pulls over. The cop's big Dodge cruiser noses up behind his bumper. He clicks off the ignition and winces as he watches the heavy-set state patrolman—dressed in a brown uniform with a trooper's hat—saunter toward him.

"Yeah, I know, I know," he blurts through the open window with a chuckle before the cop even says a word. "Going way too fast."

"You can say that again," the man chides through pursed lips.

"I hardly realized it," he says apologetically. "I mean—the Keys highway. It's so straight. And scenic. With the ocean on both sides, and all..."

"Y'know, we're just tryin' to keep these roads safe," the cop interrupts with a rehearsed tone. He sniffs the air a couple of times. "Doing eighty-three in a fifty zone isn't exactly what we have in mind." The cop scans the passenger's seat, scattered with splayed Texaco road maps, empty Styrofoam coffee cups, crumpled wrappers from burger joints, a half-finished jumbo box of Sugar Babies.

"Any reason you're driving barefoot?" the cop asks.

He shrugs.

"I'd get some sandals or shoes on, if I was you."

He considers making a smart remark, something about being a carefree beachboy and not having any need for shoes, but then he thinks better of it.

The cop steps to the back of the car, eyes his Wisconsin plates, then saunters back. "I see you got out-of-state plates."

"Um, yeah," he replies. "It's winter up there," he adds, as if that was some sort of rationalization for going that fast. "A wind chill alert, I hear."

"On some kind of road trip, are you?"

"Sure. Sort of."

"Got family back home, then?"

"I do."

"A wife or kids, maybe?"

"Um, yeah," he lies, wanting to make himself sound stable.

The cop studies his driver's license, gazes up at the highway, as if pondering the **Pass With Care** sign in the distance, then back at the driver's license. He flips up the black leather cover of his note pad with his pudgy fingers and scribbles something.

"A speedin' ticket would cost you," the cop relates. "You might end up sleeping in your van. But," he pauses, "I'm just givin' you a warnin' this time." He holds out a pink slip. "Just do me a favor, will you?"

"What's that?"

The man puffs his cheeks, slides the ticket pad into its case on his belt, hands the driver's license back to him. "I see you're pushing thirty-three." He wags his head. "Criminy. I bet your wife wants you back in one piece. You should know better than to be out speedin' like some damn teenager."

A half hour later, he checks his gas gauge. Still an eighth of a tank left. Enough to get him there—wherever there is—as long as he doesn't take any detours. The goal, he tells himself, is to get where you're going without detours. Toward the brightness. Toward the blue, the green. The colors of his future.

He needs to ride this old Volks van as far as it will go, to roll down the window, to let the gusting wind ruffle through his blonde hair, make his knit shirt flutter like a yellow wing. Even if it runs out of gas, he'd be somewhere. *Sugarloaf Key, Long Key, Big Torch Key, Scout Key, Sands Key, Knockemdown Key, Shelter Key.* More than sixty keys along Highway One, and he has them all memorized. He pictures the forty-two bridges spanning the glistening, aqua water from one sandy shore to the next; one bridge even stretches seven miles long.

Maybe he'll pull his van to a roadside at No Name Key and stay there a while; he'd pull his car to a clearing at a dead end by a beach and wait for the wind to turn the pages of his life. He'd place a line of shells on the dashboard, hang faded towels in the windows so he can sleep into the morning. Maybe there he'll begin to wear a tattered straw hat and baggy shorts; his white van would begin to turn green with a layer of fallen palm leaves. No Name Key: the slow, laid-back life, where it's always sunny and warm. No news. No wars, no economic rise or collapse, no wind chill advisories. A place where no one asks you any questions—at least not the prying kinds of questions. He needs to drown those questions like chunks of coral, to throw them far out into the deeper water, watch as the splash rises like a sudden white crown, then disappears. He'll look out over the Atlantic and see the world slipping off it, easily as a smooth waterfall dropping into nothing.

In Islamorada, his thoughts are interrupted as he sees it. He hits the brake, swerves onto the shoulder of the road and then backs up on a dirt roadside.

It's a small, empty baseball field with a line of palms and thick vegetation just beyond the small wire fence in left field. It's a kid's field— built beside an elementary school. No kids are here, though—school's out for winter vacation. The infield soil is orange. Bright orange. In the north, where he's from, the infields are tan or brown dirt. But this infield is a vivid color—a color that surprises his eyes.

He puts the stick shift in neutral, slides out, leaving the keys in the ignition. A couple of small white egrets bob up and down, searching for something on the infield. As he walks around the backstop, they tip their heads and then fly away, disappearing in the hazy blue beyond center. He steps onto the infield, its brightness startling him. When he strolls to the outfield where he notices a ragged tennis ball at the base of the rusted fence. Left behind by some kid, he figures. He picks it up, rotates it in his hand, notices its once-green color faded to gray by the sun. When he walks toward the third base line, he notices pale shell fragments between the blades of grass just beyond the chalk lines. He bends down and studies them, marveling at the thought: an entire ball field, built on a bed of coral and crushed seashells.

Near the foul line, he finds what he's looking for: a dry, bent stick— about three feet long—that's fallen from one of the overhanging trees. He jogs back to home plate. He'll hit one, he decides, just to get back that old feeling.

He tosses the faded tennis ball into the air, swings at it. Unlike a regulation bat, the stick is thin, and curved in the middle, and he misses. The ball falls to home plate, bounces a few inches, then rolls toward the backstop, its cover gathering a light layer of dust.

He notices a few clouds—with gray streaks on their underbellies—beginning to move in quickly on the horizon. Clouds he hadn't seen before.

He has to hurry, he tells himself. He can't take too much time. He needs to be back on the road. After all, the other keys wait for him. *Sunset*

48

Key. Ragged Key. No Name Key. The edge waits for him.

He tosses the ball in the air a second time, swings hard, misses again. This time the stick slips from his hands and cartwheels down the first base line. "Damn," he exhales.

He jogs out to retrieve it, brings it back to the batter's box. He wants to hit that ball. Not just wants to—he *needs* to hit it. And hit it hard. Wants to make the ball exhale a little puff of orange dust and then rise into the sky. Needs to see the ball fly over the infield and into the wavering heat, needs to see it fly over the wire fence in left, where it would land, lost in the dense grove of palms and vines and Kudzu.

But then doubts swirl in his brain: What makes him think he could hit it that far? Isn't the fence too far away, and isn't he a little out of practice, after five months of not playing? Isn't his makeshift bat— narrow as a broomstick—too awkward and misshapen? Three strikes and you're out, right?

No more questions, he tells himself. The key is to always go forward. No more pauses, no more detours. No gold rings, covered over by silt, no gas gauges or pieces of a plate skittering to the four corners. Just the color of the orange infield, so bright, bright, bright it stings his eyes. Just a man with blonde hair in white cargo shorts and a yellow shirt, standing on soil that seems to burn his bare feet.

Readying himself for the third swing, he takes a deep breath, inhales the humid air that tastes green and blue. He swings and misses again. Then again. He keeps swinging frantically until his arms and shoulders ache. His timing's off, and inertia pulls the ball to the ground each time with a vague popping sound, like the wind softly knocked out of someone. He pauses, and during that pause he feels something on his wrist.

It's a drop of liquid.

Another drop splatters near his elbow. Then a third. He notices the heavy gray cloud front sliding overhead, a thick eyelid closing over the sun. It's an oncoming storm. The wind picks up, sends a swirling gust toward home plate. The sharp palm leaves around the perimeter of the field rustle and hiss and sway, cutting the air.

He tips his head toward the sky, and a sudden cloudburst begins. The liquid rolls down his cheeks and drops from his chin to the scuffed home plate. It's just rain, he tells himself, not tears. Just a few drops of ordinary rain.

WING TIP SHOES

An hour before dusk, after a long road trip across the dusty county highways of rural Iowa, the first thing my father would do was step out of his old Rambler, raise his arms in the air to stretch his sore back, and call, "You ready? Let's go."

Waiting on the cool concrete of the front porch steps, I'd grab the two gloves next to me—one a small kid's glove, which fit my eight-year-old hand, and my father's bigger glove—a '50s style mitt with swollen leather fingers. Then I'd lift the wooden baseball bat and ball, jump down the steps, and run toward him in my tennies before he could even close the door of his Rambler, its pale green tailfins pointing skyward.

Still dressed in his white salesman's shirt, his red and blue striped tie and dress slacks, he'd walk with me across the street toward the vacant lot to the oval shape of dirt worn into the grass. His legs—still stiff from the day-long repetition of moving from clutch to brake to accelerator and back again—seemed to limp a little as he walked. On the sandlot, a rough rectangular board served as home plate. Although it wasn't a regulation plate, like the kind made of solid rubber with a bright white center trimmed in black, that warped board was always curved like a smile.

As we strolled through the long grass that warm, humid evening, I glanced down and saw that he was still wearing his dress shoes. They were wing tips, reddish brown, and still polished after his three days on the road. The shoes seemed round as the earth, and their curved tops were covered with tiny holes like stars without light, like the dull galaxy of small towns he had visited all across Iowa, their gray grain elevators at the edge of town blotting out the afternoon sun. Working for a meager paycheck, he was a traveling salesman for Nutrena. The sales job was never quite right for him, though his face lit up at each stop, and his sales pitch was as enthusiastic as he could muster, considering he was selling fifty-pound bags of dog food or grain for cud-chewing cattle caught in narrow stalls.

"How'd you do?" Mom would always ask when he'd step into the foyer of our small bungalo after a road trip.

"Sold a little here, a little there," he'd reply illusively, referring to the small commission he received from his sales.

"Enough?" Mom asked, not liking the vagueness of his reply.

"Enough," he'd echo, and then lift the brown felt fedora from his head, the shadow on his forehead erasing itself.

Maybe that's why our escape to the baseball field became a ritual each time he returned. Maybe, after those long hours of sitting on a sagging car seat, his knees ached, and the muscles in his back felt like taut wires, and he needed to stretch them. He need to slide a cushioned glove on his hand and step lightly onto the emerald island of the sandlot field.

Each week he'd be gone three or four days on county roads to towns with names like Algona and Pocahantas and Eldon and Decora—town names that, though they probably weren't that distant, sounded, to me, so foreign and so far away. I often tried to envision those places, their main streets—flat, and like a wide sheet of cardboard that would fold in on you at night. I pictured him, driving in that Rambler to the other side of the world.

"He'll be back," my mother would whisper some evenings to me, my sister and younger brother, her voice unable to hide the trembling. "Soon. He's in Cedar Falls tonight." When I pictured Cedar Falls, I imagined my father, pulling his car next to a waterfall that thundered and churned at its base, the town's perimeter surrounded by a grove of trees so dense he'd get lost in them. In reality, he was just closing the musty drapes and pulling back the chenille bedspread in the cramped Royale De-lite Motel as the red neon tubes buzzed and flickered outside the picture window. In reality, he was exhausted, his spine aching from the weight of the dozens of *No thanks* he heard each day. He was closing his eyes to rest in that darkly-paneled room, though his mind was still spinning with the thoughts of contacts he could make the following day after he woke early and gulped a cup of Courtesy Coffee from the hotplate. He was thinking of his odds of making a sale or two as he shaved while staring at the tiny waterfall pouring weakly from the faucet to the yellowed bathroom sink. Later, in the corner phone booth, silver coins would fall one by one into the pay phone as he called the local businesses. His income depended on how many deals he closed, how many he lost, and I sometimes thought that when he dreamed, he must have dreamed of grain, pouring and pouring from burlap bags like bits of dusty gold.

Once we reached our designated positions in the vacant lot—my father, standing next to the two-by-six home plate, me, near second base—he loosened his tie, slid on his thick leather glove, and rounded out its pocket with his knuckles. He picked up the ball, cradled it, and stared at it a few seconds like someone making a wish. He circled his right arm once, a windmill. At that moment, to me, he looked like a pro ballplayer, like some kind of baseball hero about to throw a ninety-mile-an-hour pitch. "I've waited for this," he said, his lips lifting to a smile, "A long time."

Then he tossed the ball to me with an awkward twist of his elbow. It was as if his arm muscles were surprised by the sudden motion, as if they were so used to steadying a steering wheel across the county roads of Iowa that they couldn't bend that quickly. The ball rose in a rainbow arc, but his aim was a few feet off; I jabbed at it with my glove—missing it, of course.

We missed a lot of things those years: My mother, anchored in the grass of the back yard by the garden on a powder blue blanket, missed my father, who would often be gone a week at a time. We missed him, too, those summers—three kids, playing for hours in the wooden sandbox behind the house, scraping scratched toy cars along a hand-made roadway toward a miniature castle that would be washed away by the first rain.

As I jogged to retrieve the ball behind me, I heard him call "Sorry. My fault."

I quickly turned and called back to him. "No, *my* fault." It was the language of ballplayers. Without saying any more, we each knew what the other meant: no one was to blame. There was no right or wrong in a game of catch on a sandlot, no winners or losers. If you dropped a ball, you'd just pick it up again. If you tossed it off target, maybe you'd throw straight to the pocket the next time. It was a humble language, and a language of belief.

We were filled with belief as we sped into the new decade of the 1960s. America was pushing at its seams; the television told us that *Progress is our most important product*, cars were getting sleeker and longer, and people were buzzing about the space race between America and the Russians. "Those little satellites are just the beginning," my father proclaimed once at dinner as we watched the flickering evening news on the black and white Motorola, "Mark my words." He set his fork on the edge of the plate with a confident click. "We'll be first to put a man in space. Maybe even on the moon someday." Mom and I nodded in agreement, and we pictured Dad's future out there ahead of him, bright and glistening as a water mirage in the heat of July on the freshly-tarred Iowa roads.

I lost some of that belief, eight years later, when I was fifteen and anxious to try out for the varsity team. One Saturday morning, I asked my father to hit some fly balls to me.

We hadn't played ball together in years, but I could recall, when I was a little kid, the way he hit some towering fly balls at the vacant field near our rental house. A reddish, leaning wood-slat fence bordered that lot, and, after our game of catch, he told me to step aside, and he'd whip the bat around and hit a few. As the ball rose, it looked to me as if it was going to stay up there in the sky. The long flies came down, eventually, close to that distant wood slat fence, or just over it, amid the saplings that led to the thicker woods. If he hit it just right, the ball would actually strike the side of that fence with an echoing *clack*. Once, playing with neighborhood kids, I noticed a fresh crack in one slat of the fence, and I was sure that one of my father's long drives had broken it like a rib. He always seemed to hit the ball farther than it ever imagined it could go, even if the wind shifted and began gusting toward us from across the field.

With those memories in mind, I strolled down Oak Street with him, ready for some outfield practice before tryouts. This time, rather than stepping aside, I planned to catch a few of his well-hit fly balls. The sandlot where we once played was long gone, of course—a new green and crème rambler-style house sprung up in its place. We followed the sidewalk down the steep hill that led to the city athletic field along the river, him in a pale long-sleeved shirt and gray flannel slacks, me in a T-shirt with my *Thunderbirds* high school logo, pinstriped baseball pants and my newly-purchased black baseball cleats.

I jogged out to medium-deep left field and he stepped next to home plate—my Hank Aaron model Louisville Slugger on his shoulder, a small pyramid of baseballs on the infield dirt beside him. Before we left, he had donned some too-white Converse sneakers that didn't seem to fit, and he looked uncomfortable as he stood there, leaning his weight from one foot to the other.

He tossed the first ball into the air in front of him, whipped the bat around, and missed. He tossed a second one, missed it again. I noticed how short and truncated his swing had become, compared to the fluid, quick swings I remembered back when I was a eight-year-old. During the years of riding in a car from town to town, he'd packed on the baggage of middle age, his body thickening, his thin chest now round and barrel-shaped. By the time I was fifteen, he had already lost a string of sales jobs after he was let go from Nutrena. As a kid, when Dad told us excitedly about each new job, I pictured it to be the best one ever— far better than the one before it. Dusty bags of feed were replaced by clean white washing machines, which were replaced by the amazing electronic ovals of Zenith hearing aids. That job was replaced by a job with Banthrico Company—where he sold dull bronze children's banks shaped like Model Ts and Abraham Lincoln and the White House. "Everybody has to save for the future," he assured us at the dinner table after he got that job, and—not able to understand the way his dreams were deflating—I nodded in agreement. Little did I know that his car's odometer turned over one-hundred thousand, all those zeros staring at him from the dashboard, and that each new venture was nothing more than a mirage that replaced the previous one. The companies always downsized, or changed sales destricts, or went bankrupt.

By the time I was a senior in high school, he'd given up on traveling sales work, and instead spent his days scanning the wavering distance for customers as he stood on the asphalt of the used car lot at Town's Edge Motors amid the dull hulls of used cars. Sometimes, on Saturday afternoons on the way to the lake, I'd cruise past the lot in my souped-up Chevy with my high school buddies. "Hey," one of the guys once blurted as I pulled up to the stoplight. "Isn't that your old man out there? He selling junkers now, or what?" My face flushed red with embarrassment. Without glancing toward the lot or answering, I just accelerated hard the instant the light turned green.

As I waited for a fly ball in the outfield, Dad swung a third time and hit a ground ball that bounced toward me; I charged it and scooped it up and whipped it back toward him. Then he hit another ground ball. Then another. After the fourth grounder, I just let the ball roll to a stop and didn't bother to field it. Frustrated, I took a few steps closer, smacked my glove with my fist and shouted impatiently, "C'mon. I want some fly balls, Dad! Not grounders. *Fly balls!*"

He didn't say anything, just paused a few seconds, studying the bat in his right hand, the baseball in his left, trying to focus and regain his timing. Then he swung hard at another one, struck it with the lower half of the bat again, sending the ball rolling slowly across the infield grass. His uppercut swing made it look like he was trying to hit one to the moon, but all he hit was grounders. For the next few minutes he just kept swinging and swinging, each time sending trickling bouncers that sputtered and stopped before they even reached me.

After a while, I thought I heard him grumble "Enough," and he waved me in. As I jogged toward him, I noticed he looked winded, his face and the ever-expanding bald spot on the top of his head turning red. He winced, shook his head, nodded at the bat. "Not so easy to hit fly balls," he muttered. "You lose the knack. Got to hit them just right, I guess."

Those two sentences were his version of an apology. It was as much as he could say to explain his weak grounders, his inability to hit even one single fly ball for his over-eager outfielder son.

I'm not sure how I replied. I might have blurted out something vaguely sarcastic, like "Yeah. I s'pose."

Or maybe I didn't reply at all. Maybe I just shrugged and scowled. That might have been enough for a teen-aged son to say about his disappointment in his father—the man who couldn't hold a steady job, the man who suddenly seemed so much older, so out of shape, and so far away. Though I eventually came to understand the frustrations of his life years later, that day I sauntered back to the house with him in silence. I glanced at the way his now-stocky body pressed at the seams of his dress shirt, the sweat stains beneath the arms, the green outline of the pack of Kools Menthol cigarettes—that he believed were harmless-showing through the breast pocket.

But that evening when I was eight and we played catch in the sandlot when I was eight, our lips curled into soft grins that never left our faces. We'd both caught a few and dropped a few, we'd both thrown some accurate throws and some wild pitches, and that was all right with us. Afterwards, on the way back, I looked down to see his wingtip shoes. I would remember those shoes for a long time—not a baseball hero's cleats, but the shoes of a hardworking, optimistic salesman, the small holes in them like the craters on the moon. I'd remember those shoes, coated with a layer of dust from kicking up the dirt near home plate. As he stepped through the deeper grass at the edge of the field, they made a soft sighing sound.

And for an hour that evening as we played, there was only a father, and a son. There was only baseball. There was only a scuffed leather ball, tracing a line in the air from his palm to my palm. Before dusk enveloped the field, there was only the curving arc of a game of catch beneath the curving arc of the azure sky above us and—I imagined—beyond that, a broad dome of thousands of unseen stars. There were only these things. And there was so much more.

IN THE MIDDLE OF A STEAL

"This one's a steal, kids," he says to the young couple, though he knows it's not true. He leans his big palm on the hood of a well-used late '80s Oldsmobile Toronado; the bright slanting morning light makes him squint, the lines and creases in his face fighting against one another. When he lifts his right hand from the hood, the stiff bones in his wrist crackle like a pitcher throwing a baseball after a long absence. For an instant, that old pain in his arm returns, then he pushes it away. "Just look at that styling," he tells them. "It's classic." He knows the robin's egg blue paint on this beast is rusting from the inside, knows most customers dislike the trunk—it's not streamlined, but cut off at an odd angle. But, for some reason, the kids seem interested in the car, so he aims one more strike to finish them off: "Best bargain on four wheels on the whole damn lot." Lately he's begun to hate not telling the truth; lately he hates the lying more than anything.

He's Dusty Sikarsky, number one car salesman in the town of El Dorado, Kansas, population thirteen thousand and something, a town named after the legendary City of Gold in South America, a place where the chief covered himself in gold dust, floated out on a lake in a raft, then threw gold objects into the water as offerings. Thirty years ago, he was Dusty Sikarsky, number one pitcher for the Kansas City Royals and runner-up for the Cy Young Award, but he never brings that up, not to anyone. He hides that inside, though it kind of eats away at him, day by day.

His fellow workers at Cashman's Lo-Priced American Auto rib him once in a while about putting on the weight or losing his hair. *What's all this talk about getting old and losing your youth?* Dusty wonders after they joke with him. *It's always somewhere inside you. Isn't it? Like some baseball covered in deep grass—all you need to do is reach down and pull it out. Right?* Mornings, the salesmen—their pompadours combed—stand shoulder to shoulder in their camel suits and trench coats, waiting for customers. Sometimes they crack a few jokes, and then go into a long pause and gaze beyond of the big front window for the first buyers, the stale smell of rising cigarette smoke mixing with the sinking scent of *Brut* cologne.

Now, on the lot, Dusty slides into the driver's seat of the Toronado in his navy suit, and, with his usual enthusiasm, rattles off the options for the young couple: power steering, tilt wheel, air, stereo radio, and even, in a car this old, a power seat that moves back and forth with the touch of a fingertip. He presses the cool chrome button to demonstrate, and it slides his weight forward.

Remembering his fingers pressing on the white leather of a base-ball, Dusty pauses in his sales spiel. For an instant, he's holding the runner on first with a frozen stare. His next pitch would be a fast one—it'd burn a hole through the air, like those satellites reentering the atmosphere. No one could dare steal second, not with his quick motion toward home, the ball popping in the catcher's mitt before the batter or runner even realized it had left his hand. Thirty years ago Dusty could have fired one past any hitter in the majors. "Sheese, you could throw a lamb chop past a wolf," a coach once remarked. Now he's firing sales pitches at customers, and at the pudgy faces of sales reps in musty Comfort Inn conference rooms. Today—wearing a plastic *Dustin* name tag old man Wenzel makes him pin to his lapel—he's pitching curves and sliders at young newlyweds like these two who stand here, lost in the used car lot, blinking at him. *The motion,* he thinks. *So fluid and decisive. Where'd it go? Who stole it from me?*

"So the price is sort of fixed, huh?" the boy asks, bringing Dusty back. The Toronado's windshield reappears in front of him, and Dusty sees, again, that almost imperceptible crack in the corner his boss told him not to mention to customers. Dusty slides out of the Toronado, pretends to peer at the sticker, though he knows the price by heart since this dinosaur's been taking up space on the lot for months. Seven-hundred fifty.

"Yeah," Dusty finally answers. "Fixed." He looks down at the rear tires, three quarters worn already, the tread thinning. He wonders if they'll have enough traction during the first sleet storm come November.

He glances up at the couple, newlyweds, and they remind Dusty of himself and his ex-wife, April, just after they got married. Everything was ahead of them then—everything was new sets of clinking dishes, the hum of their own washer and a drier, a little apartment on the outskirts of Appleton with a view of a spindly oak that spiraled upward into the blue.

Then Dusty sees the back of April's pale, robin's egg blue blouse as she walks out the door, carrying a small hard-sided suitcase, and the images fade, as if someone spilled liquid over a freshly-painted water color.

"It's got a lotta miles on it," the boy says, scratching the side of his face where his retro too-long sideburn ends at his sharp cheekbone. He stuffs his hands into his dark blue jeans. "Don't know if we can afford seven-fifty."

"So when did you kids get married?" Dusty asks, shifting the focus off the vehicle and onto something personal.

"Two weeks ago," the skinny boy says, flipping a lock of his thin, longish brown hair away from his right eye. The pointed features of his face soften as he glances at the girl.

"Yeah," the girl agrees, starry-eyed, pivoting toward the boy in her denim shirt with washed-out embroidery on it. She looks to be only about eighteen, and her almost-pretty face focuses itself on her dark red lipstick, smeared on way too thick. Her blue jeans are tight, two whitish spots worn on the cheeks. "And we might be moving pretty soon," she adds, "You know—towing our stuff across the country. A honeymoon, kinda."

Dusty pictures them, their belongings piled in the expansive back seat as they head for some exciting destination: the coast of Oregon or California. He thinks of himself and April, driving around the country in that trusty Buick Regal as Dusty moved up through the minor leagues back in the '80s. Wichita, with its flat landscape pulled taut. Then Sioux Falls. The green seas of corn rows seemed to ripple and bow and part for that car as they crossed the plains.

"So, you're road tripping, then?" Dusty asks.

"Yeah," the boy says. "But it'll cost us. We're pretty much broke," The girl nods with him. "Seven fifty's a lot."

"Well, then, maybe sleep on it." It's what Dusty was taught to say in one of the dreary sales training conferences with his boss, Dick Wenzel, a cousin of Zeke Cashman, who owns the place. "Tomorrow's another day. Come back then, and we'll see what we can do."

Gravel crackling beneath his shiny leather shoes, Dusty shuffles back to the office. For the first time in fifteen years, he begins to think how easily he could dislike this job. He doesn't relish pushing these out-of-fashion beasts he can't really believe in. You convince a few customers that a car's worth more than it really is, that it's golden, the

American Dream Machine, and then you cash in. It's the American way. But what about the buyers? Where does it get them, except a few miles down the road and maybe an overheated radiator, the Prestone, like green blood, dripping in a puddle that'll stain the pavement for years?

"Sell that damn Toronado?" old man Wenzel, his boss, barks when Dusty slips back into the makeshift office, which is nothing more than a long corrugated shed, a leaning tin island afloat on a sea of black asphalt.

"Nope," says Dusty, rubbing his hands together, though they're not cold. "Not yet."

"That's no way to get a commission, Sikarsky," Wenzel snaps. His wiry body—pinned to a wooden office chair—swivels toward Dusty.

"It'll move, eventually," Dusty replies, peering through the dust-caked picture window and into the lot, where the early morning steam rises in wisps.

"Should of never taken that piece of junk as a trade-in," Wenzel growls, taking a drag of his Camel and puffing the pungent smoke out in a oval shape. "The thing's obsolete. Better off in the goddamn junkyard."

"Hey," counters Dusty, "Give it time. It'll sell. It's got four wheels, like any other car. Just give it a chance."

In gray sweats and a billowing vinyl navy jacket, Dusty stands behind the pitcher's mound, watching Randy, a young pitcher, warm up for the seven p.m. Junior Babe Ruth League game. The kid is his prime starter on the team, a fourteen-year-old with potential. The kid may not be the next Nolan Ryan, but he could be really good. Clutching an invisible ball, Dusty goes into his stretch. "Here's how you hold a runner on so they can't steal," he says, glaring toward first base. Then he swings his arm down in his pitching motion, tossing a handful of air toward the plate.

"Now try it again," Dusty says. "But this time hold that glove to your chest just a second longer. That way, you make them doubt themselves. They have no idea if you're going to throw to first or not."

The boy stretches, then throws. It's a lame fast ball, way outside, and he hangs his head.

"Reach way back before you throw, Randy," Dusty suggests, reaching his arm behind him to demonstrate. When he does, he can feel his tendons sting. "Think of yourself as a magician, kid. You're plucking the ball out of thin air and tossing it past the batter before he knows what happened." Dusty chews on his lip for a second, then adds "Picture yourself throwing a good pitch ninety-nine out of a hundred times. And maybe it'll happen."

Randy tries it and throws another pitch. This one's faster, clipping the outside corner.

"Better," says Dusty, "Better." *With his knack, the kid could go someplace,* Dusty thinks. *If I can only make him believe in himself.* If Dusty's learned one thing about coaching, it's that—you always have to sell the kids on themselves, convince them they're worth it, because they never believe it enough. And if they believe it, they just might find out they're better than they ever thought they were.

Using his imaginary baseball, Dusty demonstrates a couple more moves for Randy.

"Throw one," a voice suddenly blurts. It's the 12-year-old catcher, Doug, a chunky kid with a balloon-round face, calling from behind home plate.

Dusty turns his head, wondering who the kid's talking to.

"Come on," Doug demands. He stands, his eyes trained on Dusty. "Throw a *real* pitch." He points to his plump catcher's mitt.

"Yeah, throw a couple," some of the other kids chime in. They pause in their warm-ups, turn and face Dusty. They look ninety-nine percent innocent as they blink at him. Randy tosses Dusty the baseball. Dusty scowls at the ball in his fist like it was a time bomb about to explode. Then he drops it to the coarse sand of the mound. "Hey. I gotta scorecard to fill out," he finally mumbles, and he strolls toward the bench, leaving the kids scratching their heads.

"Aw, Jeese," whines the catcher, flopping his glove down on the grass and following Dusty. "Why won't you ever pitch for us? I mean, you were in the *Majors.*"

"Was," exhales Dusty as he picks up an equipment bag, the bats clunking inside the sagging canvas. He pulls out a clip board with the scorecard on it. "That's the key word. *Was.* It's ancient history." He looks up at the boys' disappointed faces. "What are you waitin' for?" he barks. "Let's get some batting practice in."

On his way home from practice, Dusty pictures himself in the Majors, before the injury, and he sees his pitches, threads of light sliding right through the eyelet of a needle. He threw that accurate pitch nine-ty-nine times out of a hundred, his pitching coach told him. He pic-tures his hand, sewn to April's as they walked to the movies on Sunday nights. His hand, soft after a game, touching the back of her neck as he drove the two of them home.

Then, with a wince, Dusty recalls the injury that one cold night after a few years of stardom in the Majors.

As he threw a hard slider, he felt something separate inside his arm. He was certain he could hear a tiny bone snap with a click, like a faraway light switch. At the time he thought it was nothing. Nothing. But when he threw the next pitch, and the next, the pain spread quickly, burning in his fingertips like flash powder, a burning that radiated up through his arm, to the rest of his body and, eventually, deeper, all the way to his soul.

In the weeks that followed, his ninety nine out of a hundred dropped down to sixty or seventy, and the batters were hitting his pitches all over the damn park. His pitching coach told him they'd start using him as a reliever toward the end of the games. Even then, he could barely get through the eighth or ninth without giving up some runs. As his earned run average climbed and he was benched in favor of other pitchers, Dusty felt his glittering dreams, sinking down to some murky bottom.

At home, he walked numbly from room to room. He and April began to argue all the time. First it was small things: who left the margarine out, who didn't close the window when it rained, a plugged-up sink.

Then, after he got released from the team, it was bigger things: where their lives were taking them. What their future held now that he wasn't in the Majors anymore. Their golden marriage began to tarnish. When he defended a couple of dead-end mundane jobs he'd taken, like working at a loading dock and selling insurance door to door, April said to him, "You're not the same, Dusty. It's like you're asleep." *Control,* Dusty thinks as he unlocks the door to his apartment; that's what a person needs most. *Control. To be able to aim something and make it go right where you want it.* He takes a deep breath. *But where do I want it to go now?* he asks himself. He pictures himself throwing a baseball, sees it rise high into the azure and cirrus-streaked sky, then fall, steadily and slowly, and finally land with a scraping bounce on the oil-stained asphalt lot of Cashman's Lo-Priced American Auto.

As Dusty eats his TV dinner from a tray in his apartment, the pudgy catcher's words bounce back and forth inside his skull: *Throw a real pitch.* Dusty wonders, for a moment, what might happen if he'd try to throw a few pitches—after all, he hasn't pitched a ball for over a decade. He stands crumples the aluminum cover from the TV dinner, then tosses it toward the trash bin. It bounces off the rim and onto the floor. *No,* Dusty tells himself. *I won't throw. I won't ever throw again.*

The only place Dusty does throw is in his recurring dream. Some nights, dressed in his Royals uniform again, he peers in for his sign, nods, and whips the ball to the plate. The spinning ball follows the line his fingertips draw, right to the pocket, and explodes there, a strike. He throws another one, then another, but by the fourth pitch, his throws begin to veer off the plate. They're inside. High. In the dirt. It becomes hard work, hefting that ball that suddenly feels heavier and heavier, like a shot put. Dusty walks three men, and, with the bases loaded, the runner at third suddenly breaks to steal home. Dusty throws the ball, and instead zipping to the plate, it floats toward the catcher slowly, a weightless asteroid tumbling in space, and the runner easily reaches home before the ball even gets there. Dusty always wakes at just that moment, with the runner stepping on home plate before his achingly slow pitch lands in the catcher's mitt.

The next morning the young couple stroll up to the Toronado on the lot again. Watching them through the picture window of the showroom, Dusty can tell they love each other, just by the way they hold hands, their fingers interlocked with each other: it's not a habit, a routine. It's real.

Real, like April and I used to be, he thinks. *Until baseball stole the time we should have had together.* She left Kansas after their divorce, and he heard recently that she was in Missouri now, still single and living with her sister.

"Hey, kids," Dusty calls, as he saunters up to them in his tan suit with the sharp paisley tie. He lifts one wing tipped shoe to the bumper of the Toronado and says, squinting a sleepy eye: "She looks better than the day before, doesn't she?"

"Kinda," the boy says weakly, so Dusty knows he's got a hesitation. "But the price doesn't look any different."

Dusty thinks about this a moment as he ponders the asphalt at the back lot, and how it leads out to a John Deere dealership and then to Highway 54, which leads to the interstate, and points west. The cars just keep swishing by on that highway, he thinks, and lately it seems like no one slows or turns off to this little town.

"Well. How does an even six-fifty sound?" Dusty offers. "That knocks a whole hundred off." He knows he's got to move this Toronado because he just picked up a couple of used cars from the nearby town of Augusta, and he better make room for them or the John Deere manager will come strutting over again and tell him to keep their damn units off his lot.

"We'd probably take it," the boy says, chewing one lip, making his gaunt face even thinner, "but not for more than four hundred."

"Hey, tough bargaining," Dusty retorts. "I'll give that some thought. Have to talk to my boss, too." Dusty wrings a smile from his lips. He'd let them have the car for four hundred—a fair deal for a machine that needs new rubber and stalls at intersections half the time when he drives it downtown to Mae's Café for lunch—but he can't. Wenzel's Rules of Order. Wenzel has told him a dozen times that he's got to report back if he's giving any discounts. "Remember, make 'em sweat," the old man instructed Dusty when he hired him. Then he added his favorite sayings: "Make 'em think they've got no choice. They *have* to buy, even if they don't want to." He always nodded in agreement with himself. "That's the secret."

A few minutes later, after stopping at the office, Dusty comes back with the verdict: Six hundred. "Boss is a stickler," he tells the two. "Won't go any lower."

"Six hundred's too much," the boy says through the side of his mouth. "We can't afford it. And besides, it's a rip-off, kinda."

Inside, Dusty knows the kid's right, and he has no comeback. It's The American Way. Gouge the customer, get yourself rich. He wants to tell the boy that he agrees with him, wants to sympathetically put his hand on his shoulder, even. But instead he just stands there, feeling like something stalled at an intersection.

During the pause, Dusty sees the sinking look on their faces, can tell they need this car, but the extra money would set them back plenty. Pictures all the macaroni and cheese or *Hamburger Helper* they'll be eating for dinner in some dingy apartment over by the tracks.

Pictures a small kitchen with no dining table. Then, for an instant, another image replaces those—he sees the two of them, making love in a bed, their lips pressed together in an open-mouthed kiss, their naked bodies intertwined. *Business*, Dusty, he reminds himself. *Business*. The vision fades from his eyes and suddenly the two are slouched there in front of him, fully dressed in their denims, their dry lips pinched shut. The girl's eyelids, with the too-thick mascara, twitch. Then the two of them turn and walk away.

The next morning, as he gets ready for work, Dusty finds the the phone number of the young couple on his desk and calls them. "Stop down at the lot," he tells the boy. "I need to talk to you again."

Dusty sees them lingering near the back of the lot and he strides over. Out of nowhere, he pulls the jingling keys out of the breast pocket of his white dress shirt, hands them to the boy.

"You can have the Toronado," Dusty says.

"*Have* it? What do you mean?"

"It's yours."

"Huh?" the boy exhales. He tosses Dusty a quizzical look. "Think of it as a steal." Dusty chuckles a little as he says it, but he means it. The look on the boy's face shifts from skeptical to just plain puzzled.

"Go ahead," Dusty insists. "Drive her away." He nods to the car with a half-smile. "I filled it up with a tank of gas, even. No strings."

The girl grabs the boy's arm with both hands and sort of bobs up and down. Her red lipstick grin stretches for at least a mile.

"Finally sell that sucker?" Wenzel asks as Dusty slides up to his desk in his swivel chair. Wenzel poises his wiry body over Dusty's ledgers like a scruffy crow on a telephone wire.

"Yep," replies Dusty.

"Get the whole damn six hundred?" Wenzel rasps suspiciously, pointing a bony finger at Dusty.

"Wouldn't take any less."

"Good, good." Says Wenzel. "Cause I just picked up a used Dodge, cheap. We'll slide it right in that empty slot. It's got a few transmission problems, maybe. But shoot, we won't tell the buyers that." He laughs a wheezy laugh. "It still runs. Maybe you can unload that one next."

Dusty goes through the motions, writes up a pink invoice for old man Wenzel, but he'll put the damn six hundred into the till out of his own pocket. So what if he takes a little loss? He tells himself. Maybe some losses are worth it.

In the late afternoon, after Wenzel's left and he's alone in the office, Dusty balls up the invoice, then pauses there a few seconds, staring out at the expanse of asphalt like he's looking a runner back to third.

That evening, when Dusty lies in bed, he can't fall asleep. He keeps thinking about that young couple in the Toronado with the new set of tires he swapped from another car on the lot. Thinks about the two of them, sitting sit close together like a couple of starry-eyed junior high kids. He pictures them, passing the paint-chipped city limits sign, parting the layers of low fog on the highway, then driving all the way across America.

He should have done that with April. He should have forgotten his obsessive workouts that winter after his arm injury. He should have known he'd never make it back to the Majors. He should have tried to start over—just jumped in the car with her and driven south, out of the cold, wind-blown Kansas winter to someplace warm. Instead he stole away to the gym each morning, as she watched him leave, trying to hide the hurt look on her face.

Then he pictures the look of disappointment on Randy and the other boys' faces two days ago when he refused to pitch for them. *Maybe I'm stealing from them, too, he thinks, and I don't even know it.*

Even though it's already past midnight, Dusty climbs out of bed, throws on his sweats, and hurries out the front door. He's got to clear his mind. In the darkness, he jogs the few blocks to the ball field.

Panting, and a little out of breath, he reaches the batter's box and studies home plate: its slanted edges begin the lines that lead toward first and third, and then on to the horizon. Then he pictures himself quitting his job at Cashman's Lo-Priced American Auto tomorrow morning. Pictures walking up to Wenzel's desk on Friday morning, snapping his laminated *Hello, I'm Dustin* name tag on the coffee and red ink-stained blotter. No matter how much Wenzel rants and tells him he'll regret this, he'll shoulder through that tinny screen door of the office, let it snap shut behind him, and not come back. He knows there's something better for him out there: a job that doesn't involve selling, like that opening for a city rec center director he noticed in the paper yesterday.

Tonight, near the home team's bench, Dusty bumps his foot into something. He looks down: it's a baseball, and in the moonlight, its brown leather looks like a rusted shot put, a worn planet. Some kid must have forgotten it there after practice. He picks the ball up. It fits easily in his hand, and it's lighter than he thought it would be.

Strolling to the mound, he stands there a few seconds, hesitating. He goes into a slow stretch, pretends to throw the ball toward the plate. No, he thinks. *Don't pretend. Throw it. Throw the damn ball. No more stealing from yourself.*

He stretches again, throws a soft one, and it carves a curved shape over the plate. He chuckles at his weak, off-target throw *That one's a strike*, he thinks, *if the batter's ten feet tall, that is.*

He jogs to the backstop to retrieve the ball. He goes into the stretch and pretends to check the phantom runner at first. He throws a few in the moonlight, each one over the plate, or close enough. Even though his arm begins to ache like a bruise, it still feels good to throw a ball again. Not just good, but great. *What am I looking for?* he asks himself. *The dream's right here, in my hands.*

Then he thinks about practice Saturday morning, how the boys on his Babe Ruth team will watch from the first and third baselines as Dusty demonstrates a few pitches for them. He'll reach his arm back as far as he can—all the way to the horizon—and throw curves and sliders and two-seam fastballs to the assistant coach.

He can already imagine his pitches, slicing the corners of the plate. Each one faster and more accurate than the one before. And he pictures the boys from the team, Randy and Doug and the rest, staring in amazement like he's some kind of magician, their eyes blinking and blinking as though they—and Dusty, too—are just waking, refreshed, from a long sleep.

SOMETHING ABOUT THE EVENLY CUT LAWN

When I was fourteen, I was a weed in the middle of my father's evenly cut lawn.

Every two weeks, always at 5:15, after work, he mowed the grass of the three-fourths acre yard behind our house. He never failed to pace the yard carefully, precisely, corner to corner, not missing any spots. He followed the mower, marching behind the push bar as if it was leading him somewhere important, though, in my mind, it only led him back and forth on a cramped rectangle. Afterwards, he'd bend to one knee to pull the weeds along the edge of the aluminum shed where the mower didn't reach, his frayed beige gloves tugging at the long green shoots until they gasped and finally tore loose.

That spring, lawns were the last thing on my mind. Instead, I focused on the upcoming baseball tryouts, a few attractive girls in my ninth-grade class, and, eventually, getting my driver's license. I always pictured myself, picking up a girl in my convertible—which I didn't have—and driving them to a game where I was the star shortstop, quick and agile and making amazing plays. It would be a game I'd win in the ninth inning with a long home run that pulled the local town fans to their feet. That year, I often pictured that towering fly ball, and the dent it would make on the scoreboard, the dent it would make on the world.

I spent summer afternoons practicing with a baseball trainer called a Pitchback. It was a black elastic net strung between an aluminum frame, and when you threw a ball at it, it bounced back toward you. I'd toss a baseball at that rectangle for hours, the ball zipping back toward my glove, or off to one side so I could leap to catch it. My father always warned me to keep clear of the shed on the south end of the lot. Its sides were thin aluminum, painted a sky-blue color that faded from the sun a little each year. That ten-by-twelve-foot shed was one of Dad's prize possessions, since he kept the stocky Briggs and Stratton lawn mower, the bulging bags of fertilizer, and his rakes and shovels inside. He also stored a rifle with a scope in there, kept under lock and key in a case.

From the kitchen window, he watched me, bouncing the ball off the Pitchback. When I'd walk back into the house, my *Rangers* T-shirt stained with sweat, he'd look up from fixing a clock or a woodworking project, shake his head and mutter, "Well there's another hour wasted."

I wanted to reply with something like, "Not wasted. I'll make it in baseball someday. You'll see, and you'll be sorry." Instead I shouldered past him, tossing my leather glove onto the back wall of the closet in my bedroom.

We both knew he could have volunteered to play catch with me on Saturday or Sunday afternoons, but it seemed like he always had other things to do: there was a crinkled newspaper he needed to straighten in front of his face, a two-by-four board to saw in his garage workshop, an article to read in *Popular Science* Magazine. After all, it was his weekend off from working at the refinery on the edge of town—a place where smokestacks billowed out pungent sulfuric smoke and turned the sky yellow. And there was always a lawn mower to clean, all that grass stuck beneath it darkening into a green paste. He'd tip the mower onto its side on the driveway and spray the garden hose at the underside, circling it around and around, the same way the blades circled around and around as he mowed the yard, his heels pivoting on the corners like some sergeant marching in the military. That's what he became when he enlisted in the Army during the Korean War, he often reminded my mother and me—an officer, commanding a platoon of troops during his stint. He lost some of the men under his command, my mother told me, and that bothered him a lot. "Sometimes he takes it out on himself," she confided. He was wounded once by a piece shrapnel while he was over there, though he didn't talk at all about that or the lost troops. Mom warned that he would get moody if those topics were ever brought up.

After he was done with washing the mower, he'd roll it, still dripping emerald-colored drops, back to the corner of the garage to its proper place, cleaned and primed and ready for the next green uprising.

Some evenings, after he was done mowing, he'd sit on the porch and admire the lawn. It was as though he was in love with his lawn. It was his baby, his offspring. His back yard was the place that he could make orderly and regular, with just a couple of hours of work and a little weed-pulling afterwards. It was the place he could make exactly how he wanted it: a neat rectangle, nothing out of place. Corners as clean and sharp as a newly-made military cot in the barracks. I often chuckled to myself, thinking that if he had a good pair of scissors, he might just kneel out there and make every sure blade was exactly the same height.

That year, when I was in ninth grade, I was his little rebellion. I was the one who didn't always listen to his orders, who smoked stolen cigarettes with my buddies in the narrow space between the A & P store and Kluge's Gas, the clouds of weed smoke rising between the concrete block walls until they were whisked away by the breeze. I was the one who gulped beers, or shots of *Korbel* brandy—which I sneaked from his liquor cabinet—some Friday nights after my buddies and I hitched a ride out to Devil's Lake. The one who skipped English or science class once in a while, figuring I didn't really need them. The one who grew my hair a little too long, who quit the paper route I'd had since grade school and shunned a job offer as a weekend bagger at a Cashwise grocery store. The one who dreamed of the Major Leagues, dreamed of a big contract offer and casually dropping the letter on the kitchen table in front of him as he sat sipping lemonade and reading his morning newspaper. It would all come to me. I was convinced of that.

I did mow the lawn with him many times, of course. On Saturday afternoons before dinner, his stern stare convinced me. When I finished the back half, tasting pungent exhaust from the sputtering muffler and the salty sweat that boiled from my forehead, I passed the mower to him, waiting for me in his faded khaki tank top. He took the push bar and finished the front lawn that led to the street, where people would see it as they walked or drove by. As I let go the push bar and the mower rolled toward him, we didn't talk during the exchange. The roar of the motor was too loud. And there was nothing to be said anyway, except maybe one-word utterances: "Here," or "Okay."

After he cut the front, he killed the motor, and I figured we were done. I turned toward the house, and as I did, he held the beige gloves toward me. "Do the weeds," he commanded.

"Why do you bother with them?" I asked.

He fixed his gaze on me, his eyes suddenly hardening into pale blue stone. "Job's not done until they're gone."

"Why not just leave 'em?" I countered, knowing I was treading on his territory now, but saying it anyway. "They'll just grow back."

"The place would look ragged. That's why." His voice tightened a little, like the wires of a clothesline with too much weight hanging on it.

"So what if it did?" I said under my breath.

As if it was an answer, he took a step toward me, lifted the stained gloves and held them right up to my face so I could smell the musty soil on them. It was his way of saying *Just pull the damn weeds*, and I knew that. So I grabbed the gloves, slid them on, and stomped back toward the shed. As if they'd been lying in a bed of thistles or poison ivy, the gloves seemed scratchy on my hands as I pulled the weeds hastily, clods of dirt still clinging to their roots. I threw them down hard with a thump.

Those gloves didn't feel the way my baseball glove did. The smooth, oiled leather always felt like it belonged there as I snagged the ball from the Pitchback. I knew some day I'd trade those ugly, pilled garden gloves for a Major Leaguer's batting gloves. Knew someday I'd caress the soft cheek of a girl with my strong hand. I was sure that if I stepped into the rectangular batter's box in the ninth on some crucial game, that I could knock the ball out of the park.

Then there was that day, while my father was in the house, when I hit a stone with the mower. The whirling blades sent it shooting, rocket-like, toward the shed. It struck the side with a low-pitched *clunk*. Making sure he wasn't looking out the window, I cut the power on the mower and jogged over to assess the damage. Sure enough, the stone put a solid round dent—about the size of my fist—into the side of his shed. As I stared at the indentation, I smirked. I thought of how the rock flew like one of my line drive base hits: solid and hard and uncatchable. That evening, after dinner, while Mom was clacking the dishes in the sink, he confronted me. "There's a dent," he began casually, his voice flat, "in the shed." He kept his eyes on a newspaper, opened to the ad page. His teeth were too close together as he said the words and they hissed a little.

"Oh?" I said, feigning innocence. *His precious shed*, I thought.

"You do that with your baseball?" He accused, not taking his eyes off the paper.

"Huh? Nope."

"Then what happened?"

I let my shoulders lift into a shrug. I was wearing a polyester baseball jersey, and could feel the heat rising on the back of my neck.

"I think you know," he said through a puffed breath. "You and your damn Pitchback."

"Didn't do it with the Pitchback," I countered.

He finally lifted his eyes from the paper, and they burned into me. "Then how'd it *get* there?"

"Dunno," I replied. "Maybe some kids in the neighborhood did it. You know—delinquents." I pronounced the last word slowly, so it verged on sarcasm. He was always complaining about juvenile de*linq*uents and how they needed to be reined in. He claimed they needed structure, and that their parents should send them to the military. That would shape them up, he claimed.

He didn't say any more after that. His eyes just slid back to the newspaper, still scanning—I figured—the ads from the hardware store for new lawn equipment. Garden Weasels. Miracle-Gro. Hose retractors. Weed-Begone. Then he lowered the paper to the kitchen table and stood slowly. As he pivoted, his back stiff, and stepped out the door, I noticed the corner of the paper soaking up some of the black coffee he'd spilled in the saucer.

Through the parted the drapes, I watched him—hands on his hips in his taupe gardening slacks and his off-white T-shirt—staring at the dent in the shed. I knew he was probably assessing the basic science of it—the size and velocity of the object that might have struck it. The angle from which it was propelled. The trajectory. He leaned really close to it, examining it, as if he was looking for any indentations that might resemble the seams of a baseball. Then he straightened, his back stiff as though it was made of steel, strode toward the door of the shed, pulled on the handle, and disappeared inside.

In a few seconds, I heard the sound. *Pow.*

Then another one, and another. *Pow. Pow.*

The sound reminded me of muffled explosions, and it unnerved me. I saw an alarmed look fill Mom's face. She rose to her tiptoes and peered out the window toward the shed. "What's that?" she gasped.

The sound continued, and, squinting, I finally noticed the dent, popping steadily outward. He strode back out, holding an old hammer with a wooden handle—the one with the thick rusted nail in the top to keep the head from flying off. He bent to his knees to check the dent, which was almost gone, though it was still uneven. It couldn't be smoothed over completely; we both knew that. Then he reached up and ran his index finger gently around the ripples in the tin as if he was touching a wound.

That spring of freshman year, at the baseball tryouts at the high school field, I tried to field the grounders and the line drives the coach hit to me. A couple of years practicing with the Pitchback prepared me for that, I had thought, though the coach's hits were faster and harder, and I bobbled a couple of them. My throws to first were off target, one of them skipping in the dirt and hitting the first baseman in the shins. I noticed the coach and his assistant in the dugout, making notes on a clipboard.

During the batting session, we had to bat against a pitching machine. None of us guys had seen one of those before; the machine's metal arm circled around, scooped a baseball from a wire chute, and, after a slight pause, flung it suddenly toward home.

I dug into the batter's box, leveled my bat confidently across the plate, and waited. The arm swung down and the first pitch hissed past me as I whiffed at it. Then I missed the second one. I couldn't get my timing right. The circling metal arm distracted me, kept me off balance.

Out of the dozen pitches allotted to each batter, I only hit three or four wimpy ground balls. After the practice, the coach rounded up the two dozen boys by the dugout. He told us there were only enough uniforms for eighteen players on the roster, and he was sorry if our name didn't get called. Then, one by one, he called a kid's name, and that kid jumped up and grabbed a jersey from a mothball-scented cardboard box. I sat there on the hard bench, edgy, as name after name was called. Finally, after calling seventeen names, the coach was down to the last person who would make the team. He scanned the remaining row of boys a few seconds, then focused on the clipboard. I sat there, feeling every grain and splinter in that wooden bench beneath me. The coach mumbled something to the assistant, who nodded. Then he looked up and announced the last name. A kid sitting next to me leaped up. I felt the air knocked from my lungs from the deep dent in the middle of my chest.

I stood from the bench, my glove dangling by its strap from my index finger. I wanted to just throw the glove across the hard gravel of the infield and leave it there.

Just then I looked up toward the bleachers. There sat my father, on a bowed plank in the top row. He'd been watching the tryouts all along.

I didn't want to go anywhere near him, just wanted to stomp home by myself, but he motioned me over with a solemn tip of his chin. He stepped down the planks of the bleachers and I shuffled up to the other side of the wire backstop. I could feel the failure that seemed to coat my skin like a thick layer.

"Hey," he said to me through the corroded wires.

I didn't reply.

"So much for tryouts, eh?" Then he gave me a slightly sympathetic look, an expression I'd rarely seen. He must have read the pain on my face.

Still, I didn't say anything to him. There were no words that could explain what I was going through. The fantasy of my ninth-inning heroics faded. I felt the dream inside me crumpling; the batter's box closed in on me, squeezing me, crushing me.

I turned to walk away, but then his voice stopped me.

"You know," he said, "I got cut from the high school football squad. Not big enough for a lineman, the coach said, and too slow to be a running back." He pinched his lips into a tight smile. "Worst day of my life. At least at the time. Until the war." He scratched the side of his receding hairline, then added "The next year I reinvented myself as a defensive back. And finally made the team."

"Oh," I exhaled.

"And you can do the same. Keep practicing. Who knows? Maybe you'll get better. You just have to work at it."

For the next few hours, I thought about his words, played them through my head again and again.

At five-fifteen that day, we mowed the lawn—me cutting the back half as usual, him the front.

Later, that evening, I stood at the kitchen screen door, watching him from behind. He sat in a sagging lawn chair on the porch and gazed out at the freshly cut lawn in the dusk. I began to understand that maybe I wasn't his disappointment—his weed, his unruly plant bristling up among the soft blades. Maybe I was more like the thin, tentative, slim-rooted grass blade in that bare spot in the soil that he watched from afar. Maybe he wished he had tended it more, pulled the enoaching weeds from around it, watered it more frequently.

I'd never done it before, but that night, after shouldering through the screen door, I handed him a glass of lemonade and lowered myself to the lawn chair next to him. "Looks good," he probably wanted to exhale with a sigh, but instead he was silent. Without speaking, both of us just stared out at the expanse of grass, a low layer of fog beginning to drift over it. I glanced over at him and he nodded, not really to me, or to the lawn, but to something else, and for some reason I nodded along with him.

SWIMMING THE QUARRY

Every morning, when Bud Walden wakes, he thinks about clear spring water and tombstones.

All his life, Bud's heard the stories that the water in the town of Cold Spring, just off County Highway 66, is like some kind of fountain of youth, but he's not sure he believes them anymore. People say the local water filters through so many layers of granite that when the springs make their way back up to the surface, they're pure as anything you've ever tasted. He's heard that people around here stay younger because of the quarries. As a kid, Bud often swam in the deep, spring-filled granite quarries surrounded by high piles of sharp-edged rock. *Best water in the Midwest*, everyone in town will tell you, *best in the whole USA*. The legends claim that if you drink it often enough, you'll feel it pouring down to that deep place inside you, where nothing else ever reaches— that healing place. And you'll suddenly feel like you could live a long time. Bud's heard all those stories, but since his wife died last year, he's not at all sure about them.

Walking downtown to meet his buddy Shorty Kohlbeck at the Cold Spring Tavern, Bud catches a glimpse of himself in the Rexall drugstore's big window: he's wearing his usual coach's outfit—a white knit shirt with *Bud* embroidered in red on the left side, slacks, and a blue *Rocks* warm-up jacket. He looks sporty, but a little overweight where the jacket bulges at the front and sides. And his hair looks thinner on top, a little more of it jumping ship each morning as he showers. "What the heck—it's only hair," he chuckled to his barber, as Ned spun him around in the barber's chair. In the mirrors on opposite sides of the wall, Bud saw an image of himself—white cloth pulled up to his neck—repeating itself into the distance. Still, he decides he doesn't look bad for a retired guy.

Then he shifts his thoughts to the Coach's Regional Baseball Conference in two weeks, where he's scheduled to deliver the keynote address. "Just talk a little about life, Bud," said Mickey Laudner, head of The Businessmen's Club, a guy who always wears some kind of cologne and a camel trench coat, summer or winter. "Sheeze—it should be a snap. You been coaching for two decades now. You got all the wisdom in the world." But Bud doesn't know what he'll say. He doesn't know how to begin to summarize a team, a season, a life.

At least once every baseball season, reporters from the city make a trip on County 66 to Cold Spring to interview Bud about his townball team. Since 1934, the Cold Spring *Rocks* have been to the state tournaments over fifty times, winning the Minnesota state championship nearly a dozen times. The team takes on high-powered squads from Rochester or the Minneapolis suburbs, but somehow they still come out on top. The reporters from the city always want answers; they want to know why, for the past sixty years, a little town of only a couple thousand people keeps turning out championship teams. And each year, Bud thinks hard and long about giving them an answer, but he can never come up with a good one. Sometimes he considers blurting what Shorty always says, something like "It's the water," but he knows that the reporters, dressed in their navy sport coats and ties, would scowl at a flip answer like that. So instead he makes up something that might sound okay in print. "It's the determination," he told a reporter a last year, tipping his *Rocks* cap back on his forehead for emphasis. "When you're small, you have to be real big inside."

Later, when he reads the articles in the *The Minneapolis Star-Tribune* or the local papers, Bud chuckles to himself as he gets to the quote because it sounds so good. He's glad they didn't ask him the follow-up question—"But there are *hundreds* of small-town baseball teams in this state with determination, and they never even make it near the state tourneys, so *why Cold Spring?*"

"Do you believe what you said in that article?" his wife Shirleen asked him a couple years ago, before she became ill. They sat in the living room of their small house, Shirleen's feet resting on a purple embroidered footstool.

"Heck no," Bud replied. He leaned back on the beige La-Z-Boy.

"Then what makes the teams here so good?" she asked. "What do you *really* think it is?" She brushed her brown hair, graying in streaks, behind one ear. Bud always liked that gesture, the way, after all these years, it still made her look casual but sexy, the way it made her look like a teen-aged girl peering into the rear view mirror again.

Bud chuckled. "Now you sound just like one of those dang reporters."

"I'm not trying to put you on the spot, Bud," she said. "I just want to know. I mean, they've won a lot of games while you've been coaching, and I understand that. But why did they win so many championships even *before* you coached?"

Bud shook his head side to side, peered at the plaques on the wall commemorating his league championships. "You can't think too much about things," he finally said. "If you try too hard to explain something, maybe you'll ruin it." For Bud, it was like analyzing the angle of your arm just at the moment you're throwing the ball toward home plate. Nine times out of ten, your muscles will tighten and the pitch won't go where it's aimed. The ball will skip on the dirt and bounce past the plate.

"Come on, Bud," Shirleen coaxed in her smooth English teacher's voice. Thirty years of teaching, and the students loved her. She was a thin woman, but strong, and expected a lot from her students. Whether it was Allen Ginsberg or Wordsworth, she always made them think. "Tell me what you're keeping inside. Just *try* to explain it to me." Her blue-eyed stare ate through him. It always did.

He sat silent for a few seconds. Sometimes the right words just didn't come to Bud, and he always wished they would. He waited for them. It was like shouting a word or two across a pond and then waiting for the echo that never bounced off a granite wall on the far side. Maybe it was a handicap, he often thought. Or maybe not. Then he stood, walked over and kissed Shirleen on the cheek.

"Bud," she said, her face flushing as she laughed that musical laugh. "You're not answering my question."

"I just did," he replied.

The memory drains from his mind as Bud reaches the corner of Main and Quarry Street and slips through the warped aluminum front door of the Cold Spring Tavern. Inside, the greasy scent of a grill and a deep fryer wafts toward him. Burgers. Fries. Fish.

Shorty Kohlbeck, a former granite worker, is already sitting on a red vinyl bar stool that matches his red flannel shirt. He's ready for the Friday night fish fry. His scrawny, five-foot two grasshopper-like frame fidgets on the stool. He pushes a bottle of beer toward Bud. "Yer late," Shorty says with a thin-lipped grin. "Almost had to take care of this one myself."

Bud chuckles, takes a slurp from his bottle of Cold Spring Beer, the local brewery. Shorty reaches into a crumpled brown paper bag, pulls out a donut hole, pops it into his mouth. Even though he's an ex-high school shop teacher, Bud feels more comfortable hanging out with guys like Shorty than he does with the teacher types, who always seem to be thinking too much.

"So, you got the speech all planned out for that conference?" Shorty asks, leaning toward Bud. The bluish smoke in the room seems to rest in a layer on the oil-speckled brim of Shorty's blue *Ford* cap.

"Not exactly," says Bud, propping his elbows on the wooden bar.

"Just saw the program," says Shorty. His suspenders hug his small, bony shoulders. "Says you're a keynote speaker. *Cold Spring Baseball Over the Decades*, it says. So what the heck you gonna say?"

"I'll think of something," Bud replies, tucking his knit shirt into the sides of his pants. He hates the way, as he gains weight around the middle, the shirt seems to keep coming untucked all day.

"I got it," spouts Shorty, slapping his small palm on the bar, circled with rings from years of glasses and bottles. "Why don't you recite Eddie Gaedel's batting statistics?"

Bud tips his head back and laughs. Shorty always makes Bud laugh, and he likes that.

"I suppose I could do that," agrees Bud, running his hand through his receding silvery hair that's slicked back. Shorty's referring to one of his heroes from the '50s, a little person who was sent in as a pinch hitter in the Major Leagues for the St. Louis Browns. Gaedel had only one at-bat, walking on four pitches, all of them above his head. Later he was quoted as saying "I felt like Babe Ruth out there."

"Or how about 'The life and times of Shorty Kohlbeck?'" Bud quips. "You know—just a *short* speech."

"Yeah," says Shorty, ignoring Bud's humor. "You could do an Eddie Gaedel tribute. Say something like, he was luckiest man on the face of the earth. And also the shortest." Shorty chortles at the thoughts. "Speaking of luck," he says, turning to the bartender, "Gimmie another of those Cabin Fever tickets, will you?" The bartender slides one of the lottery tickets onto the bar. "You know there's a million dollar prize in one of these?" Shorty says to Bud, who nods. "You bet," he continues, "just match three walleyes, and scratch off a million in the box in the corner, and it's all yours. Imagine," he says, raising his voice over the whine of the Hank Williams Jr. song, "a million bucks!"

At seven o'clock, Bud pauses in the doorway of the tavern, waves goodbye to Shorty. Shorty waves back, then leans over the bar, pondering the open windows of his losing lottery ticket. "Damn crappie," Shorty mutters. "Why the hell couldn't there be *three* walleyes?"

A little dizzy from the beer, Bud heads for home. As he walks down Main, he passes the whitewashed sign painted on the brown brick side of the hardware store:

Welcome to Cold Spring, Home of the Wonderful Waters

He pictures himself, swimming in one of the clear, water-filled quarries as a kid. He'd go there often to cool down on hot summer days, jump from a ledge, the water splashing like a transparent wing. Then he'd swim to the center and tread water there, the clear eye of the pond staring up at him as he stared at the sky. He and Shirleen went there a few times the summer after their senior year, and they'd tread water, facing each other in the rippling liquid.

When he reaches St. Stanislaus Catholic Church on the corner, something tells him to pause there.

Standing in front of the church, constructed of huge cubes of gray granite, Bud can almost smell the dankness that surrounds the place. He realizes that the last time he was in this church was at his wife's funeral, a whole year ago.

That year seems like a lifetime. He pulls on the large, heavy wooden door, stiff on its hinges. Inside, the church is dim, except for the pink votive candles, lit for the lost souls, on the side of the altar. He squints down the row of thick marble pillars, and, along the walls, sees the statues of the saints in their long, flowing plaster robes. He studies the Gothic altar, its white pinnacles topped with gold spires and silver stars. When an image of his wife's coffin, draped in flowers, flashes through his mind, all his thoughts suddenly stop.

He leans against a wooden pew. He's waiting for something: a thought, a feeling. Instead, nothing. Nothing comes into his mind. The votive candles don't even flicker; they just toss the steady rounded shadows of their opaque red glass jars onto the plaster wall. Lately, just when he thinks he might need them most, no thoughts come into his head at all.

Bud hurries out of the church and past the cemetery without looking at the gravestones, those dark, crooked teeth sticking up from the
jaw of the land. He knows Shirleen's is one of those. Fourth quadrant,
ninth row in the corner, closest to the lilacs.

When he reaches his small house, he steps into the back yard and
takes a few deep breaths, calming himself. He stares out at the land to
the west, flat all the way to the horizon, ponders the fact that the whole
town's built on a huge shelf of granite. A *ledge*, the quarry people call it,
as if it's something you could fall off. It's under Main Street, it's under
the broken down wood frame houses with tin roofs and the leaning
porches, it's under the baseball field where his team plays. Sometimes,
at practice, he thumps a bat on the ground around home plate and it
sounds sort of hollow. It bothers him when realizes there's an empty
space down there in the granite, beneath the succulent grass.

"Somethin' wrong, coach?" one of the players asked him last spring
as he watched Bud tap the bat on the orange dirt of the batter's box and
stand there, bent at the shoulders, listening.

"Nope," Bud had replied. He put the bat back on his shoulders,
checked his watch, and turned toward the boy. "Hey, it's almost game
time. Better start warming up."

The next day, as Bud drives his Mercury to the ball field for practice,
he passes the granite works. Gray and pink speckled tombstones line
the highway near the works—rows and rows and rows of them, waiting
to be shipped to cemeteries. Everyone in town knows this tombstone
business supports the town's economy. It's the water, everyone says, and
the granite shelf the water filters through. Every day the slabs are loaded
into railroad cars, their sides rusty and pockmarked with dents, and the
boxcars trundle down the tracks on their way out of town. This town
has supplied tombstones to nearly every town in the country, Mickey
Laudner once bragged.

At practice, the *Rocks* boys still look rough. Bud's a quiet but firm
coach, and the boys thrive under his guidance. They'll be ready when
the season starts, but today their fielding's off, missing ground balls,
dropping flies in the outfield, and throwing offline. Afterwards, they
hang their heads, upset by their poor play.

"Patience," Bud tells the boys afterwards in a team meeting as he leans near home plate on a 36-inch Louisville Slugger fungo bat. "The three Ps are practice, patience and more practice." Then he adds his favorite story and quote. "When a famous ballplayer made a great catch in the outfield, his opponent, passing him after the inning, said 'That was just *luck*.' And the guy replied: 'The more I practice, the luckier I get.'"

Near noon, Bud parks his car downtown and some townspeople wave and nod at him with a proud, knowing look. He strolls past the Springs Soda Fountain that advertises **Ice Cream and Live Bait,** then steps into the Rexall drugstore, picks up the morning paper, and on the front page is the news about another car crash on Highway 66. Bud's all too aware that Cold Spring is known for something else besides its granite, its water, and its baseball teams—it's also known for the car accidents that always seem to occur on the small County Highway 66 that leads to and from town. Everyone knows there are more head-on collisions, more one-car rollovers, more fatalities on 66 than on the interstate and all the nearby country roads put together. That two-lane road is flat, and relatively free of curves and blind bends, yet people are killed there often, and it doesn't matter if it's high noon and sunny or the moonless pitch dark of 2:00 a.m.—every couple of months, Bud sees another feature on the local news page of a mangled car, the rescue crew in white, a body covered and blurred on the roadside. *Why that road?* Bud wonders. *Why's there so damn much death around here?*

"Suicide sixty-six," Shorty calls it. So do some of the other residents, including the mechanics at the Townsedge 66, who rotate the tires on Bud's Mercury once in a while. Sometimes Johnny, a poker-faced mechanic, will say, "You got a bulge in the right rear, Bud." Or "Them brakes are thinning out. Wouldn't take that thing out on suicide Sixty-Six." So Bud always gets the problem fixed, there on the spot. He doesn't take the chance. And he knows Johnny isn't just putting the screws to him when he finds something wrong; he's just telling it like it is. When you've towed as many smashed cars as he has, the crumpled front ends raised high as if in terror and the windshields spoked with spider webs where someone's skull dashed against it, you start to think a little more cautiously. All that has taught Bud to be just a little nervous about things. Lately Bud has the distinct feeling that when things are good for too long, the balance lever tips and they're bound to change. *But why that highway?* Bud wonders. *Why always just outside Cold Spring?*

"It's the granite shelves beneath it," Shorty muses philosophically between bites of his boneless perch at the fish fry the next Friday night. "It's that gol-damn granite."

"How do you mean?" Bud inquires, wondering what kind of hare- brained idea Shorty's come up with tonight.

"Welp, here's my theory," says Shorty, trying to sound intellectual. "The granite shelf gives off a kinda radiation, see, just like the Bermuda Triangle or something." His tiny fingers clutch the bottle of beer, his eyebrows fold over his brow, and his oversized facial features look larger as he bends toward a *Lucky Sevens* pull tab he's just bought. Bud thinks about how, when Shorty holds still, he could be a gnome, a plaster dwarf statue on someone's lawn. "This here's the Cold Spring Triangle," he continues, tracing a triangular shape on the bar with his fingers. "Causes craziness, poor judgment. Shoot—people feel like they can do any damn thing. Think they can drive 85 or 90, passing cars all the way to gol-darn North Dakota. Then they meet some damn fool coming the other direction who's thinking the same thing. Then shit, it's all over." Shorty squints one eye and pulls a thin white bone from his lips. "So much for boneless," he mumbles, tossing it to a napkin.

Later that evening, on the way back from the bar, Bud finds himself kneeling in the pew of the empty St. Stanislaus Church. He recalls that time when he was in grade school, and one boy from his third-grade class was hit by a semi on County 66 while riding his bike on the shoulder. No one, not the nuns, not even his mother, could explain why it happened. He was just a kid, the classmates said, so why did God let him die? The Franciscan nuns simply quieted the class with their pat answers, like "It was God's will," and then folded their arms beneath the starched white panels on the front of their habits. He remembers, in third grade, realizing how many deaths and tragedies happened that no one could explain: infants dying in cribs, whole villages swallowed by earthquakes, famines, pandemics.

Tonight, a wavering image of his wife's coffin appears in his mind, then disappears. The statues of the saints, lining the altar, don't have any answers, their faces stoic as the huge stone faces on Easter Island that Bud saw once on television, faces that stare out at the endless water and keep their secrets to themselves.

"Life's short," blurts Shorty in the bar, a couple of beers making him feel moderately witty. One of his eyebrows raises, like a caterpillar climbing a tree branch. He orders another bottle of Cold Springs, a couple pull tabs, and two Cabin Fever lottery tickets.

"You've got that right," remarks Bud. He knows what Shorty means: a week has passed already. The boxes on the calendar seem to blur from Friday to Friday. Time never slows down; it only speeds up, like some runaway train heading—steadily faster and faster—toward the horizon.

"So you gotta grab what you can," adds Shorty. He reaches into his crumpled bag of donut holes next to him on the empty bar stool. "I guess that's the secret. Right, coach?"

"Dunno." Bud closes his eyes, inhales a whistling breath through his nose. The two sit for a few seconds without talking, Charlie Daniels' fiddle music jittering from the juke box.

"So," Shorty slurs, then sucks on his lips. "Coach's conference is tomorrow. What the heck you gonna talk about in your speech?" He leans close to Bud's face, so close Bud can see the pockmarked craters of his acne scars from forty years ago.

"How 'bout the Eddie Gaedel story?" Bud says with a smile.

Shorty just shrugs. "His record in the majors was zero for zero, ya know. He batted just once, but when he walked, it goes on the record books as zero for zero." He wags his head side to side. "It's like he never existed." He squints at his two lottery tickets, scrapes the silver coating off them with a nickel. Neither of them is a winner. He breaks into a high-pitched cackling laugh. "Damn, I'm lucky," he says. He turns to Bud with his crumpled bag from the bakery. "Want a hole? I got a couple left."

The next morning, Bud wakes before dawn, fixes his coffee in the aluminum percolator. He sits with a pencil and a blank sheet of paper in front of him on the table, stares out the kitchen window at the pinholes of stars, fading as the sun rises. This afternoon, the coach's conference will be held in in a meeting room of the Holiday Inn in Saint Cloud, a nearby city. The wallpapered, thick-carpeted meeting room will be decked out with vases with plastic flowers on each table where the young, pretty waitresses shuttle back and forth with juicy steaks and ice clinking in their pitchers of water. All the important people will be there, including reporters from the *Minneapolis Star-Tribune*, the Twins vice president, and even a rep from the Governor's office.

Bud gazes at the paper, wishes Shirleen were here now to help him write this speech. "Speak from down deep, Bud," she might say. "Let your real self come out, that inner part. It's like an underground spring. It'll help you say what you need to say."

He knows the reporters from Minneapolis will approach him with notebooks and recorders, asking him the usual question—"How can a little team from a town of two-thousand do so well?" Bud's going to try to prepare some answers. *When you're little, you have to think of yourself as...* Naw, he tells himself. They've heard those clichés before. It's got to be something else. He can't really think of the phrases that capture his philosophy. He can't really think of any words at all right now. Then, suddenly, an answer pops into his head—an answer that, if he said it during his speech, would throw everyone in the room into a gasping hush:

Some think it's all talent, but it's not, he pictures himself saying. *Some think we're invincible, but we're not. In Cold Spring, our teams play baseball on a huge, granite tombstone. In a way, we're surrounded by death. The boys are young now, they're alive, sure, but the tombstones are always waiting, just a few inches beneath the surface. Either you live with everything you've got, or you spend your life dying.*

Bud shakes his head over his coffee, thinking how strange that would sound. But, at this moment, in his mind, it seems true, the best explanation he can give. Bud almost chuckles as he thinks of the headline in the Sunday morning sports section of the *Star-Tribune*: "*Rocks*' Winning Coach Spouts Sermon About Death."

Then he ponders the other things he could say when he leans into the microphone, things he believes in his heart, things he and Shirleen talked about often, things that would draw puzzled looks from the whole audience:

We win, sure. But it's a gift, and you didn't earn it or ask for it. It's a gift, but you still have to use it right. We're just a little town, and we're lucky to have talented teams. But we can't let ourselves forget how small we all are. Let's think about that the next time we complain that our town's team isn't on a winning streak. Let's think about the underprivileged, the people who struggle with discrimination each day. Let's think about children starving in foreign lands. Let's think about the wars that tear countries and families apart. Let's remember that, around here, a lot of us middle-class folks are fortunate—we're pretty-well well fed, we have our comforts and cars and solid homes, and that a lot of people are not born so lucky.

Saturday afternoon, before the banquet, Bud slips on his knit coach's shirt, glances at the *Rocks* logo embroidered right over his heart. He tucks in the shirt, slaps on a little Aqua Velva, pauses in the doorway by the mirror, and pictures himself saying goodbye to Shirleen, the way he always did. "Don't say anything dumb to the reporters," he imagines her saying. She even said that to him when she was sick the spring before she died, her voice more husky. He remembers her hair, quickly fading to gray. Even her lips seemed to lose their pink color as she moved like a ghost through the house, the disease eating away at her. He remembers the love between them that nothing could eat away.

"I'll try not to," he'd always reply with a laugh. He always wished that he had the right words to say to her, to comfort her when she was sick. He always wished he could have said more. Instead, he simply caressed her hand with his, then, shouldering through the screen door with his clipboard, he'd pivot and toss his best smile back to her.

Though he tries to block it from his mind, for a moment the scene comes back to him: it's a year ago, and he's back from practice and calling for Shirleen, but she isn't in the house and her car—an old Galaxie she had for years—is gone, even though she hasn't driven for months. The radio on the desk is playing swing band music through a little static, and all the windows are open, the silky drapes blowing in the breeze as if she's still sitting there, tipped back in the lounge chair, waiting for him to come home. A half-hour later, he got the call from the police station about the accident. "Better get right to the hospital," the sheriff said. "A one car rollover, out near the quarries." They told him later she was heading west on 66, and it seemed, by the looks of the accident, that the car was traveling at a high rate of speed.

He stares at himself in the mirror and asks himself the question he's heard a million times before: *What was she doing out there on the road alone when she was sick? Did she veer off the road and into those boulders on purpose?* She always said she didn't want him to have to watch her die slowly. Now he tries not to imagine her, driving at 90, then suddenly letting the steering wheel go, as if you were pulling back from embracing a lover.

He hops into his Mercury and it coughs to a start. He drives down Quarry Street and, turning the corner, he sees, a block away, Shorty's old Ford pickup, stalled at the only stop sign on Main. Inside the cab, Shorty's body jerks forward and back, flopping like a hand puppet as he cranks and cranks at the engine. As Bud gets closer, he sees the air freshener shaped like a pine tree swaying from the rear view mirror. Shorty's truck finally starts with a roar, a blue globe of exhaust surrounding it. Shorty drives two blocks, pulls into the Handicapped Parking stall in front of the Cold Spring Tavern where he always parks, though he's not handicapped.

Bud pulls up alongside, rolls down his window and waves to Shorty, who steps out and props his tiny body against the brick wall beneath the flickering bar sign. He's eating a donut hole from a crumpled white paper bag.

"See you back here after the conference?" Shorty calls to Bud.

"Yeah," says Bud. "After the dust settles."

"I'm buying," says Shorty. "I'm also getting a new goddamned truck." He points to the silvery tips of lottery tickets sticking from the pocket of his red and black flannel shirt. "If I get lucky, that is."

Bud drives off in the low sun, and long shadows extend from the small houses. He thinks about how the reporters will hound him again about how many years he plans to keep coaching. They'll ask how long this small-town team can possibly keep winning. They'll be impatient, as usual, and they'll insist on a reply. "How long?" they'll ask. "How long?"

He crosses the tracks, reaches the intersection by the Townsedge 66 and pauses a few seconds. It's closing time, and the mechanics are outside, tossing bald tires in back of the concrete block building, their hands and wrists dark with grease. Johnny looks up, poker-faced, and nods at Bud.

A squad car accelerates past on 66, disappears into the pink glow of the horizon.

Bud feels his hand shift the car into reverse, and he backs his Mercury onto the shoulder of the road and clicks off the ignition. *I still have time,* he thinks.

He slides out of the car, follows the trail through the brush a quarter mile up the track bed. For a few steps, he balances on the rails, rusted on their sides, shiny on the tops from the aching, moaning loads of granite that pass over them day after day. In the distance, he can see the granite works and the piles of stone to the left side of the tracks, Highway 66 veering away on the right.

Puffing a little, Bud reaches a clearing at the bend and there it is: the spring-filled quarry. He stops, peels off his *Rocks* shirt, trousers, socks and shoes, then, in his boxers, wades into the water. It sends cold splinters into his legs, but he likes the sensation. The water beneath him is clear; he catches himself thinking—for an instant—how water that filters through so many granite shelves is always the purest. He swims toward the deeper water, his arms suddenly graceful, like wings, the liquid making him feel lighter, buoying him up the way it always felt when he swam here as a kid. Then there were the times he swam here with Shirleen when they were first dating. He imagines the two of them touching hands beneath the water. Her fingers, giving off warmth as he closed his palm around them. He feels like he could tread water here all day, all summer, all year, without ever getting tired.

The simplest answers are always the best, he thinks. The ones that come from deep down.

Forever, he'll tell the reporters when they ask him how long. *Forever*.

A DAY IN THE LIFE OF A GROUNDSKEEPER

So much depends on his small baseball field, set between the green rows of the corn field and the pale stones of the cemetery. So much depends on the way he tends the grass, watering it and watering it on the last days of summer, so it burns green as long as it possibly can. He waters it until the grass blades reach up with thin fingers to touch the leather soles of his work boots as he steps lightly across them. No matter if the people in town say he's obsessed with this field and call him an oddball, Darrin Spahn knows a lot depends on the way he bends down to check that white chalk line along the third and first base lines; he knows if he wavers the slightest bit, fair becomes foul, foul fair.

He knows that when the little leaguers from town run onto the field, it'll be ready, waiting for them. There are no bad hops on his field—it's hard enough to catch a whirring grounder without it hitting a rut and taking a vicious hop toward the face. It's hard enough to run back to the wall for a long drive without a low spot pulling the ground out from under you, throwing you off balance. Balance: that's Darrin's credo. Balance and leveling and balance.

Darrin knows he could brag about the place, but he doesn't. He could say the Randolph Memorial Field is the best-kept townball field in Minnesota, but he doesn't—he just tends the field alone, with no one watching. He pound nails into the warped boards of the outfield fence, straightening them, then covers them with a coat of whitewash. He rakes and grooms the soil around the batter's box until it's smooth as the stretched blue sky above it. He knows, as he grooms it, that he's only touching the surface, the skin of the soil. He knows the soil he touches goes deep into the earth where no mere man could ever reach: it goes all the way to the soul of this planet. At least that's what his father told him once as they sat in the grandstand. His father learned *his* from his father. Darrin's father and grandfather were groundskeepers, tending the same grass on this field in this town where all three of them grew up.

Once in a while, at dusk, after he finishes his jobs, he gets the impulse to run the bases, imagine the cheering in his ears as if he's just hit a home run that wins the World Series. But, at 77, he's too old to run like that. Instead, he sometimes drop to his knees in the middle of the diamond and give thanks for the millions of grass blades, for the chance to water them, keep them green this long into the late August drought.

He knows some people in town make fun of him, especially Colton Comstock and his two snarling buddies. They say he takes his job too seriously for what it's worth. But exactly what *is* it worth? He'll tell you what: inside those rickety wooden fences, rounded to 400 feet at their furthest point, 330 feet down the lines, is grass so green you'd swear it would live forever. Inside those fences is a diamond that—if you looked down and spotted it from one of those jet planes heading to Milwaukee or Chicago—you'd say is just right in its symmetry.

On the north side of the ball field, next to St. Joseph's Church, sits the town cemetery, and he tends that, too. He pushes a hand mower between the gravestones carefully, so as not to disturb the dead, so the place stays neat in case the living want to come to visit. Sometimes he pauses and stands in front of his father's headstone, which has been there for ten years. Next to it is his grandfather's. If he pauses there too long, feeling the vibrations in the hollow handle of the mower, the exhaust starts to burn his eyes and makes them water, and he just has to move on.

"You know you don't have to mow the cemetery," Father Francis often tells him. "You don't have to tend the graves. We could hire someone."

"I mow it because I want to, that's all," he replies. He figures you have to find the things you really like to do, things that help other people out—small as they might be—and then just go ahead and do them.

He loves to begin mowing at the outside edge of the pitcher's mound, and then circle around and around, the way his father taught him. Each circle surrounds the one he's just mowed. Sometimes when he's finished, he climbs to the top row of the bleachers and gazes out at the nap of the grass, carved in a spiral. And he thinks *Yep, that's it, all right.* He thinks about how you start with one small circle, then make a second one, a little larger than the one before. He thinks about how, eventually, you could mow around the whole planet that way, circles around circles. All the while, almost without your knowing, the sun circles across the sky and the earth circles around the sun. It's then that—feeling suddenly a little dizzy—he realizes how tiny he is, how humble we all should be, and how he's not much different than a single blade of grass circled by billions.

But not everyone is humble. Some people think the world is so small they could squash it in their hands like a piece of clay. Some nights at the Wander Back Tavern, guys like Colton Comstock remind Darrin of that. Colton sneers at him from under the shadow of his greasy ball cap, then stares back at his hand of cards, always a little bent at the corners. After a few beers, Colton starts in on him, saying "Hey Darrin, why ain't you out there cuttin' the grass with a fingernail clipper?" He lets out a laugh, which, after smoking half a pack of Marlboros, rasps from his throat. "Hey old school," his friends chime in, "why aren't you out there saying prayers for your precious grass?" Then they guffaw and high five each other.

These guys are a few years out of high school; Colton works part time at a low-level job with the county, digging roadside ditches with a Ditch Witch, and the other two are usually unemployed. Colton, who drives around with a low-slung '80s Pontiac Grand Prix with a Confederate flag in the back window, never fails to talk about how his work is a pain in the ass. Friday and Saturday nights, with nowhere to go, they hang out at the Wander Back, playing Sheepshead and shaking dice and flexing their muscles in their cutoff shirts as they lift pitchers of beer. Sometimes, for no particular reason, they start fights in the bar, especially with the Mexican workers—those temporary summer residents who pick crops on the local farms. That bothers Darrin, because he's become friends with some of those guys, especially Jose, a hard-working family man who is witty, and always quick to laugh.

As usual, Darrin ignores their comments tonight and orders a Grain Belt, which he gets, along with a sympathetic nod from Harold, the middle-aged bartender. Darrin realizes these young guys just don't understand the life of a groundskeeper. They don't know he's seen a lot of dry years when the sky held back on the rain for weeks, and he had to be out there morning and night, arranging the sprinklers. They couldn't imagine the parched dry taste in his throat those summers. They haven't been through the wet years, when the water pools around home plate and third base, and he had to cart in wheelbarrows full of dry sand just to make the infield playable for the local townball team, the Mudhens. They don't remember those years, or carry them around deep inside the way Darrin does.

"Hey Darrin. How come you don't answer?" goads Colton. "Why aren't you out there saying your prayers?"

He starts to burn as they keep it up, and he wants to burst out with "Maybe you boys should be doing something worthwhile with your lives," but instead he just takes a slow sip of beer and gazes behind the bar at the photos of the town's championship amateur teams, the bronze trophies glimmering next to them. He knows Colton and his pals were never worth a damn as ball players; they never played on the team, like some of the local boys.

Later, as he leaves the tavern and walks back past the darkened field, he hears it: the growl of an engine in the parking lot behind the grandstands, voices cackling with a sound like empty tin cans clanking together. Then he sees headlights flare at the right field corner as someone yanks the gate open. Darrin limps onto the field by the dugout and stands there, eyes fixed on the low-slung car that pulls across the right field line. *Jesus*, he thinks he says with a gasp, *Jesus!*

It stings his eyes to see the car rumble onto the outfield. Then the engine revs and it spins a circle in his grass, carving grooves with its rear tires. The headlights circle themselves as the car roars, its rear end rotating around and around. He flinches, feeling each gouge in the sod as surely as someone is scraping his skin with a dull knife.

Breaking from his trance, he hurries to the storage shed, pulls out a Louisville Slugger, and begins to walk toward the outfield. The car idles a few seconds, its exhaust rising into the red glow of its taillights.

The engine snarls and the car turns, its headlights aimed toward him. Then it accelerates right at him, faster and faster. He supposes they figure he's going to turn and run, and for an instant, he thinks he is, too. But he just holds his ground. His wiry body gathers all the strength from those years of hefting wheelbarrows and bags of chalk lime and mountains of dirt, and he just holds his ground.

The car speeds closer and closer toward him, its lights steady, not jostling at all on the surface of the grass he's taught to be so smooth. A few yards from him, the brakes wheeze and the dull chrome fender slides toward him. He wavers a little as the car finally comes to a stop just inches in front of him, and the engine kills. The passengers' rapid-fire laughter echoes off the fences.

Fists clenched on that Louisville Slugger, he squints at the grinning faces in the darkened car, illuminated by the amber light of the dash. It's no mystery about who's inside that lowriding, dented red Pontiac. He knows its Colton and his pals.

Darrin is a peaceful man, and he always has been; he's always kept to himself. But when he thinks of the burning scars the tires have cut on his field, it finally gets to him. He can almost hear that field, that innocent field, crying out to him in pain. It's then that maybe he does go a little crazy, like people have been saying.

He rears back, and like a ball player leaning into a fast ball down the heart of the plate, he takes a quick, hard swing with the wooden bat. The left headlight bursts with a hollow *pow*. The laughter inside the car stops. "Hey, goddamn it!" Colton's voice rasps, "The hell you doing?"

Doing what I need to, he thinks as he moves to the other side of the car, swings the bat and the other headlight explodes. Inside, Colton curses Darrin as he grinds the ignition and the car turns over a few times until the engine finally catches. As the car backs away, Darrin glares at the dark, blind eye sockets of the headlights. "You're gonna pay for this, old man!" he hears Colton yell out the window as he retreats and steers the car back through the gate.

Darrin can't stop his whole body from shaking, can't stop his heart from squeezing and squeezing its fist inside his chest. He stands there for a long time, gazing at his damaged field, the circular ruts he knows are out there. He's afraid to walk out to the outfield to check all the damage, afraid not to. One thing he knows for sure—whatever scars are out there, he'll carry them around with him for a long time.He thinks for a moment about those boys, pities them for their cruelty, for all that pent-up anger coiled inside them that made them do this. The way they've learned to hate people that they don't understand.

And then another thought seeps in; he's upset by what they just did, and by something else, too. He's always believed that so much depends on this field, but right now he realizes that, no matter how much he tends it, the field won't last forever; it's not perfect and he can't keep it that way. It's just grass. Just thin and fragile blades of grass.

He walks to the outfield and pauses near a circular rut that's at least two inches deep. He frowns at it, then tilts his head toward the clouded sky, and the first drops of rain gently touch his face. Then it begins to rain harder, soaking his tan shirt and pants, soaking the field and the ugly gouges left by the senseless tires. Wisps of steam rise from the raw, dark soil of the ruts as the cool water lands on them.

It's then that he falls to his knees. He reaches down, presses his palm into one of the ruts. Along its edge, he sees the tiny, pale, exposed roots. He caresses them with his fingertips, and as he does he believes can feel them, already beginning to grow.

PART THREE:
IN ANOTHER LEAGUE:
CURVES, CHANGE-UPS,
AND STOLEN BASES

THE ROMANCE OF CERTAIN ABANDONED BASEBALL FIELDS

Though the backstop of this ragged field is bent and dented, the wires still braid together in diamond shapes, like lovers who refuse to let go.

First base is a piece of plywood someone tossed down. It's only an inch thick, but has buoyed up the soles of a thousand cleats or tennis shoes. Safe, or out: those are the only two words the first base knows.

Second base is tentative, its wood warped, curled slightly by the staring sun. Wan and bleached, with a dark spiral knot in its center, it worries perpetually about its heart being stolen.

Third base whimpers. Because triples are rare, this lid from a cardboard box always feels ignored, lonely, and not touched often enough. Like the floor of a house where people rarely come to visit, it's always waiting.

The first and third base lines are mute, and undecided. If you stand at home plate and look their way, there's no chalk line to tell you whether a ball is fair or foul. You just have to know by sight, by memory, by intuition. Gaze down the line, as a twisting fly ball drops from the sky, and—like an honest umpire—try to make the right call.

The pitcher's mound is a misnomer. Here, it's not a mound at all, but a circle of flattened grass. Still, when the pitcher draws his or her arm back to throw the ball, the earth seems to rise, to arch its back. The pitcher's mound becomes the focal point, the center of the diamond, the place where the game begins, and ends, the place from which light sparkles.

The grass of the outfield is always overgrown. Always. But get used to it. It can never be tamed, can never be separated from the wild weeds or the tiny saplings that spike from it, their stalks scratching the morning sky.

The grass has learned to fight inertia, to slow a rolling baseball, to arch and bow like small breaking ocean waves, to spin itself into whirlpools, to curl into a cave for ants and beetles, a diving board for locusts that flick and spring. On hot afternoons, you can hear the sound of unseen insects clicking and buzzing. And, on still spring evenings, when the insects go silent, if you listen hard enough, you can hear the soft sighing song of the grass growing.

There are no outfield walls, of course. The field goes on forever. Forever. Forever.

The gusting wind is the owner of this field, and patrols it constantly. If the wind is calm everywhere else on earth, it will be gusting on this one small field. The wind's mission in life is to ripple your T-shirt, blow your hair into your eyes, to flip your ball cap from your head and send it cart-wheeling across the infield, making you feel foolish and small. Its mission is to rush across the infield, to summon the field's spirits from the patches of bare soil, to raise them and show them to you in whirling dust devils.

The wind can knock down the pride of any line drive. Or, if it decides to, the wind can push a ball—hit high into the outfield—farther than it ever imagined it could go.

The batter's box is not a box; it knows no corners. It's more of an oval, carved into the soil by the thousands of batters stepping into hundreds of thousands of pitches. After years of use, it has taken on the shape of an eye, as if it's looking deep into the earth.

And last but not least, the plate. What about home plate?

There is no thick, anchored black and white rubber slab here, like the ones on regulation fields. In fact, there's nothing here at all, except a worn spot, so you have to imagine home. Or you could try to duplicate it, using whatever you can find: a leather mitt, a book, a tennis shoe left by someone, a discarded high school love note held flat by four small stones, a square of sunlight. Or a slice of a dream.

Home plate: It's the place where, long after the game is over, you meet at midnight, one on each side, with your new lover. It's the place where the moonlight shines down and makes the powdery dust between you glisten at the moment you lean toward each other for that first kiss.

THE DESCENDING GOD

If you ask, he'll tell you that he wears a lucky number zero-zero on his jersey, and that he plays center field for the *Playa del Carmen Municipales* in Mexico. And he'll tell you what he wants most is to run across the field in center, to make a great diving catch, and to land in a center field filled with succulent deep grass.

But there are no green fields in the league where Hernandez plays.

Today, before the game, as he looks toward his outfield, he sees almost no grass—only clumps of stubbly green scattered around the hard-packed tan dirt of the outfield. The lonely, thick, bristly blades claw their way up into the one-hundred-degree afternoon heat on Sundays as the *Playa del Carmen Municipales* host a team from one of the smaller beach towns to the south like Akumal or Puerto Aventuras. Still, Hernandez will try his best, as he does every day. Along with the rest of the players, he's heard the rumor that an American baseball scout is in the stands to watch today's game.

Hernandez knows where the well-groomed ball fields are—in El Norte, in America, like the Red Sox Fenway Park, or the Minnesota Twins Target Field, where the grass grows to a rich, vivid color, a color that soothes your eyes just to look at it. In *El Norte*, those ball fields are watered by sprinklers each day. Sometimes he fantasizes about it: it's grass that would caress your toes as you walked through it barefoot, grass where you could lose yourself, grass where you could fall to your knees and roll, grass that's so luxuriant and succulent, you could almost die in it.

Not so here, on the Playa del Carmen municipal field—off Calle 20, blocks away from the congestion of tourists in rented minivans headed for the beach or the all-inclusive mega-resorts. Here, the infield dirt— or *el concreto*, as his best friend Jorge Castillo once called it—seems to spread, as though it were a living, growing entity, farther and farther into the outfield each year. Hernandez sometimes gazes at it and wonders if soon the whole field will be dust and pebbles, pebbles and dust.

Hernandez believes there's magic in his blood. He believes the magic comes from his Maya ancestors, centuries ago, who, before they passed from this earth, calculated the rise and fall of the sun, the rise and fall of seasons, and invented the calendar. Because of his mostly Maya ancestry, he's a small man, and tubby for an outfielder, with short arms and legs. "*El Gordo Chihuahua*," some of his teammates call him—the Chubby Chihuahua. His Maya blood gives him less agility as an outfielder than a taller, sleeker player, like some of the players with African or Spanish heritage, but he believes he makes up for it with the magic. *Magia.*

He can't throw the ball fast, but he can throw it far, and accurately; the way lightning is accurate when it chooses a place to strike. From the outfield, he can throw the ball right to the catcher's glove, see it center there, as if in the middle of the Maya calendar. Hernandez does not sprint gracefully toward a fly ball that's headed toward the wall; he trundles beneath it with his legs pumping like pistons, tracking the ball diligently, getting there in due time, with no wasted motion. He chose his number—00—for his tattered gray jersey because his Maya ancestors invented the zero.

"Why *zero zero?*" Jorge, the big first baseman with the wrap-around snake-eye sunglasses asked him.

"Because I'm nothing yet," Hernandez replied. "I'm *nada nada.* I'm still waiting to become something."

"To become what?" Jorge questioned. "What, Hernandez?"

"I don't know yet," Hernandez answered. "A Major Leaguer, maybe. A ballplayer with green grass beneath his feet."

Jorge shook his head and mumbled, "Ay, Hernandez. When will you ever learn? When will you grow up?"

Hernandez just gives his rounded shoulders a shrug.

At 42, Hernandez is the oldest man on the team, the one who sweats the most when he runs, the one who hears the air wheezing from his lungs after a short sprint to first base. But he's also the one who smiles the most, the silver edges glistening at the bottoms of his big front teeth. El Viejo—the Old One, as they sometimes refer to him—is the player with the most spirit, everyone on the team agrees, the player with the most hope. *Esperanza.*

Hope for what? Hernandez sometimes ask himself. *For what? For a green and succulent future? To dive into that future and never slow down?*

Lately, for Hernandez, time seems to speed up: the older he is, the more quickly things seem to pass. He knows that the Maya knew time well. They analyzed it, etched it in the hieroglyphs of their calendar; they calculated dates a thousand years before their existence and a thousand years after. Hernandez knows time, too, day by day, year after year, its pace quickening. An age spot here, on his forearm, another one there, on the back of his throwing hand. Some days during warm-ups he rubs a little powdery soil on the spots so they blend in.

Today, before the game, the word spread quickly through the *Municipales'* dugout: a scout for an American minor league team—affiliated with the New York Yankees—is in the grandstands for the game. He is a tall, thin man, with pale, sunburned skin, and he stands out clearly in the wooden grandstands—unlike the rest of the fans, he is wearing sporty beige shorts, a pink knit shirt and a Calvin Klein cap with the letters *NYC*. He does not shout out at the players through megaphones—fashioned of plastic quart bottles of *Coca-Cola* that were cut in half, like some of the regular fans do. The man has spoken to the *Municipales'* manager, and though the players are buzzing and excited—especially Hernandez—the manager warns them that he's not sure if the man is on a scouting mission or not. He is staying at a fancy penthouse suite in Playacar, the hotel complex with entry gates watched by guards in uniform who check each car as the tourists enter the manicured tropical grounds. The manager added that the scout doesn't drink the local *Cristal Agua*, but only *Perrier* sparkling water prepared in the USA. He did not help himself to the *Sol* or *Superior* beer bottles from the cooler beneath the grandstands, as the manager suggested. *Cervesa es libre*, the manager insisted. "The beer is free. On the house." But the scout simply declined the offer with a wave of his hand, saying he only drinks wine.

Sometimes, after the games, Hernandez sits on the top row of the bleachers with his back against the corrugated tin of the grandstand and pictures ancient priests, standing at the top of the pyramid, sacrificing something and praying to Chaac, the patron god of rain and lightning, then turning their broad, flat faces toward the sky and hoping for rain. Blood pools on the pale limestone altar, then Chaac is appeased, and the rain falls down, watering the crops, and the corn grows tall.

Sometimes Hernandez shakes his head, wondering just how much had to be sacrificed to get the rain to fall, the corn to rise to touch the sun.

Then he gazes out at the field, sees how much it needs rain this Julio, sees how parched and cracked the soil is. If you scuff your toe on the outfield it sends up a little tan cloud. Clouds of dust—not rain clouds—are all that drift over this outfield.

Yet he's proud of the field; he loves it, in all its dryness, because it's the only field he knows. He loves it, despite the broken glass that litters the left field foul line—the shards of green and brown from *Coke* and *Superior* bottles, the empty tumbling plastic bottles of *Manzanita Sol* apple juice. He loves it, despite the pieces of paper and the candy wrappers that circle crazily around themselves in the tiny whirlwinds at the corners of the park. Loves it, despite the half-foot long chunks of concrete that always seem to appear near the cement outfield wall in left, not too far from where he plays. He thinks road crews or kids might be throwing them over the outfield wall. The uneven chunks keep appearing on his field each Sunday, as if some huge wall somewhere is crumbling, piece by piece, and each Sunday Hernandez totes them toward the foul line.

"What are you today, the garbage collector?" his third baseman might quip as he notices Hernandez cleaning up the outfield.

Hernandez might grumble as he tosses a shard from a bottle into the rusted tin drum near the dugout.

Hernandez knows well the stories of how his Maya ancestors quarried huge limestone pieces and carved them into blocks. Then, even with their primitive technology, they placed one on top of another to make amazing pyramids to honor the sun and moon and the rain god. These pyramids survive in Chitchén Itzá, and in the ruins to the south of Playa like Tulum. Some pyramids stretch for the sky at a height of over one hundred sixty feet. Tourists from American Express with spindly legs, trying to climb them too fast, get heat stroke. The pale crème colored palaces rise high toward the sun, and sometimes there are tabernacles on their top platforms, and carvings of a menacing Chaac, his half-closed warrior eyes glaring, a serpent in his hand to represent lightning.

But there is a god more important to Hernandez. At the top of several pyramids is the carving of his favorite Maya image, the Descending God. The Descending God leaps from the tops of the pyramids toward the earth, his hands clasped in front of his face like a diver. His grandfather—a shaman in his village—told young Hernandez that the Descending God is diving to the spiritual world. "*In the ancient days*," his grandfather said, "*a man would dive from the top of the pyramid in a ritual sacrifice. Sometimes he took with him an offering of a lamb or a chicken.*"

When Hernandez tries to make a diving catch of an almost-out-of-reach fly ball, he has to time it just right. He has to stretch as far as he can, to make sure that the ball will land gently in the palm of his old thick-fingered leather glove. He has to make sure it sinks deep into the pocket, his bare hand clapping on top of it so the ball doesn't jar loose when his stocky body hits the hard ground and rolls once or twice. Any good ballplayer must learn to do this, he tells himself, any ballplayer worth the salt of his sweat.

But once, just once, Hernandez would like to rise up from the ground without the bloody scrapes, without the grains of sand and grit imbedded in his knees and elbows. He smiles as he rises, yet he feels himself weaken each time the blood drips from his skin. Each time it drips from his body, he loses something. Just once, Hernandez would like to leap for a ball in the outfield and then rise up stained with green, and whole, and new again.

The high priest were like spirits, his grandfather once told him—they could walk right through walls. It was amazing, how much his ancestors could do with so little—they could build huge limestone cities in the middle of the jungle flatlands where there were no indigenous stones. They were great astronomers and could calculate—to the minute—when the sun would appear on the horizon on the solstice, and when Venus would rise. "*Muy fantastico*," his grandfather exclaimed. They were proud and regal and built a great civilization, with cities of a hundred thousand that rose from the jungle. Then there are those unique, tongue-twisting Maya words, the lost language Hernandez no longer remembers. His grandfather taught him many words when he was a small boy. *Learn these words*, his grandfather said. *Learn them, remember them, use them. Kukulkan. K'ich'ean. Xpu-ha. Quetzalcoatl. Ix Chel. They will make you invincible, no matter what happens.* A few years after his grandfather died, the language was lost to Hernandez, its strange, musical sounds with its Xs and Zs and Chs, each word sizzling like cicadas hiding in the undergrowth at dusk. The words conveyed of histories, prophesies, legends, songs: words filled with magic, words filled with fire, with lightning. Hernandez always wanted to be *that* good at the game of baseball, as good as the Maya words that so adeptly described the world.

Today's Sunday afternoon game does not go well for the *Munici-pales*. The scrappy team from the neighboring resort town of Akumal beats them by the score of six to one. The *Municipales* get only two hits off a long-armed fireballing Akumal pitcher named Ruben Cortez, who everyone suspects is not just part Spanish, but also part Cuban or Dominican, like some of the great pitchers who play for the American big leagues. To add to their insult, they make five errors in the infield. Hernandez suffers a nondescript game, going 0 for 4 at the plate and fielding only three easy fly balls.

After the game, Hernandez, thirsty and soaked with sweat, unbuttons the top three buttons of his jersey, exposing a cheap gold-plated chain and a pale barrel chest, and drinks greedily from a bottle of *Sol*, pulled from the cooler where the bottles clink against melting blocks of ice in the murky water. The entryway of the grandstands is crowded with ballplayers from both teams, who laugh and drink and talk in a post-game ritual.

"I am the center fielder," Hernandez says in Spanish to Jorge and some of the other players gathered in a group. He taps his chest with his stubby index finger. "I am not the best you've seen, but I'm not the worst, either. Si?"

The players chuckle.

Then Hernandez turns and tips his head toward the sky. "Praise the sun god," he says, bowing his hands extended, "and praise the rain god."

"You and your Maya rantings," says Jorge. "You and your crazy Maya magic. You learn that from your grandfather?"

"Of course. Where else?"

Jorge shakes his head. "Soon, after one too many *Sols*, you'll claim you are the Descending God. You say that after every game."

Just then they see the American scout, making his way through the crowd, his shoulders high above the short ballplayers, his blondish hair wavy and combed back. The scout nods politely to the players who talk loudly and brag and laugh, their tipped-back ball caps sporting the names of local merchants. When Hernandez sees the man, he rushes up to him. "You did not see my best fielding," Hernandez says to him in

Spanish, and when the scout tosses a puzzled look at him, Hernandez tugs on Jorge's sleeve. He knows Jorge speaks a little English and will help him translate. "You did not see my fielding skills," he says again in Spanish, then elbows Jorge. "Tell him, amigo."

Jorge translates for Hernandez with his thick accent, and the scout shakes his head. "I'm only here on vacation," the man says, rubbing the back of his neck, which is red with sunburn. "I'm not scouting."

"*Solimente una tourista*," Jorge says.

Hernandez pulls Jorge aside. "I caught nothing but easy fly balls today," he says insistently. "I want to show the scout what I can do. I want to show him the real me."

The scout tries to brush past the two men and toward the exit gate.

"You will watch me a few minutes, no?" Hernandez says, following him. "I am the best center fielder in the Yucatán."

Jorge translates, and the scout gives him a tight-lipped smile, then shrugs, as if he doesn't really understand Jorge's translation. Then he checks his cell phone and mumbles "I have an appointment."

"Wait," Hernandez says to Jorge, sounding desperate. "Tell him I am the Descending God."

"You are loco, Hernandez."

"Tell him, Jorge. Just tell him *that*."

Jorge, too embarrassed to say something so strange to the American, but still trying to help out his old friend, says instead, "He is a god among outfielders."

"Okay, okay, what the hell," the American says reluctantly, holding up his big hand with the slender fingers. "But I've only got a minute."

Hernandez turns and hurries toward the sheet metal dugout where the wooden bats lean next to a cluster of baseballs.

"Hit me some, Jorge," Hernandez says, pulling his glove onto his thick fingers. The glove looks too small for him, like a child's, but it fits. Hernandez jogs toward center field, his rotund belly jostling.

Jorge shakes his head in resignation, sets his bottle of *Superior* on a bowed bleacher plank, and picks up a 35-inch bat. "Go ahead. Make a fool of yourself."

"*Señor* scout," Jorge says with a laugh, sweeping his hand toward Hernandez. "Let me present to you Hernandez, best outfielder we have ever seen in Playa del Carmen." Murmuring to each other, the men from both teams cluster around Jorge and the scout to watch the spectacle.

"*Mira!* Look!" one of the players who speaks English jokes. "He's can run half as fast as the Hall of Fame base stealer, Ricky Henderson." Then he adds a punchline, making the men chuckle. "He is a *half-fast* ballplayer!"

Hernandez reaches a cleat-marked spot in center, about thirty yards from the concrete chunk that's lying in the dirt near the base of the wall. He puts his hands on his knees, feet balanced apart, and nods at Jorge.

Jorge tosses the ball, sweeps the bat around, and hits a high pop up that begins to fall between second base and center. Hernandez gets a late break on the ball, runs in, and straightens up as the ball lands in front of him, bounces on the hard-packed dirt, and over his head. The men laugh as he runs the ball down, throws it weakly, but accurately, back in. "He is old," one of the men mutters to the scout in broken English. "Forty-two *anos*. He is the oldest man on the team, but he is trying to prove himself. All his life he believes he will play for the American leagues."

"Hernandez, he is not quick, but he's fast," one English-speaking player says to the scout.

Another man behind him quips, "He's not fast, but he's quick."

"Uh," the scout exhales, then takes a slow sip of his *agua pura* and checks his cell phone again.

Jorge hits a fly ball, and Hernandez gets another slow jump, then runs in too far, and the ball sails over his head.

"Ayyyyy," some of the men groan with disgust and embarrassment.

"Enough!" Jorge shouts out to Hernandez, waving him in, trying to protect him from further humiliation.

"No," Hernandez shouts, straightening his back. "No. Hit me another one. Not so easy this time. Hit me a *tough* one this time!"

"Forget it!" Jorge bellows, thumping the bat's barrel on the caked dirt. "Come in and have a beer, Hernandez. The game's over, *amigo*."

"*Una mas!*" Hernandez demands. "One more!"

"Damn him," Jorge mutters. "He's a stubborn old son of a bitch," he says, apologizing to the scout, who has already taken a step or two toward the exit gate. Jorge lifts the bat one more time and hits the ball solidly.

Hernandez sees the ball rise up into the air from the circle of men, a tiny silhouette crossing into the sun. The ball is hit right at him, but deep, deep. He turns and begins to run backwards, and for a moment, he loses the ball in the sun's glare. But he keeps running anyway, not seeing it, still somehow seeing it at the same time. He knows he must run a long way to catch this ball; he must run across centuries, across continents, across time in order to reach this one.

He is neither old nor young anymore. As he runs, he hears is the raspy sound of his own breath, hears the hush of his dulled steel cleats scraping the soil, the pounding of blood in his arteries. He hears his grandfather's voice, urging him on. He hears the faraway cheers of his teammates near the grandstand, and beyond that, faintly, he thinks he hears the chanting of his ancestors—the high priests—at the altar of the pyramid.

He keeps running and running until he wonders if maybe he's passed right through the wall—like a spirit—and is still running, beyond the stadium with its crumbling limestone and its rusting grandstands, beyond his homeland, beyond *El Norte* and all its wealth, even, and onto another field.

The ball seems to be just out of reach. Just out of reach: like everything else in this world.

Watching, Jorge takes in a quick breath and holds it.

It's then the ball begins to drop from the circle of the sun. It's then that Hernandez squints and recognizes it again: a leather sphere, a *bonita*, symmetrical planet, a world he has to catch before it falls and touches the ordinary, pebbled dirt, a world he has to catch before it self-destructs, leaving only a scuff mark, a puff of dust on the dry plain of the universe.

So he gathers all his strength and leaps, and the leap takes him farther than he has ever jumped. The slow-motion leap feels good and sure and perfect. He leaps into his future, and descends to the ground, and as he does, he takes something with him.

He takes with him a wish. It's a wish that—instead of the hard-packed soil and the chunk of concrete rising to strike his forehead—the field was made of something softer, something green and flowing, something that would embrace him after all these years. And as he comes back to earth one last time, his ancestors are there, waiting for him, smiling as they stand, surrounded by the lush blades of grass and the tall, tall corn.

A CERTAIN SMOOTHNESS AND ROUGHNESS

Lying on his back on the smooth pine bench of the dugout, he wakes to a sound. It's the distant of the boxcars, clunking as they roll away from the freight yard on the other side of town. It's a good sound, he's decided. The sound of a train whistle, its low moan tearing the sky, is a good thing.

It's a sound of going somewhere.

And the steel wheels sound right on the polished track, too, their *clack clack clack* increasing in tempo as they roll slowly away from town, all that weight of a hundred cars gathering momentum as they trundle toward the horizon.

Lonnie is sleeping in this dugout of the high school field because, he's told himself, it's as good a place to rest as any. He lies there in his worn flannel shirt, his frayed jeans, his oil-stained leather boots because the pine bench is a pleasant place to lie down and sip a can of lite beer and then doze off, the early afternoon sun slanting across the field and plying into the creases of his face.

He's just resting a little, that's all. He doesn't have too many places to go, after all, except for this dugout, and then, toward evening, to sit on a park bench, maybe, or head to the Flick's Café on Main.

At the café, he won't think about the woman he sat there with, years ago, in the sighing red vinyl booth. Years ago. She wore a silky blue dress, and the two of them sipped cups of coffee, lingered over pancakes, the syrup pooling on top of them as they talked about life and marriage and maybe a kid or two. He won't picture her face, the swirls of red hair like muted fire, all that light behind her eyes. He won't picture that. He can't. Not right now.

His memories are interrupted by the sound of the whistle again: that long, low-pitched chord. It sounds like three notes at once. A kind of music, he thinks.

He knows the sound well. He also knows that a train, headed to Fargo or Billings at full speed sometimes sounds like a scream as it passes you. He's been that close to one, standing on the crushed stones just a few feet from the tracks, feeling the ground shudder like a small earthquake, the whipping wind and dust stinging his face.

Then he closes his eyes and hears the scream of the fans from the bleachers as he hits a high, deep line drive. It's high school, 1998, and he could hit the ball hard in those days. He watches the ball rocket through the sky and sees the outfielder take a step or two and then give up as the ball traces the shape of a cloud high above the center field fence. It's the American Legion championship, and when the sky finally lets go of the ball, it bounces on the other side of the fence, the game is over, and Centerville wins the state championship.

Now, opening his eyes, he gazes at the field where, as a breeze lifts its head, the grass moves away from him in rippling waves. He thinks about how it seems like an easy thing, to hit a ball with a large-barreled piece of wood, but it's not. It seems like an easy thing to lie on the varnished pine board in a dugout in the afternoon, but it's not. The pine board is smooth, but it's splintered along the edges, too.

Nothing is so easy anymore—things are just the way they are. The pine boards and the sleeping and the cans of Lite just *are*, and so he goes with them. The woman wearing a blue dress in the red booth is gone. Right now, his muscles gone slack, his life is a rise and fall of waking and sleeping.

Tomorrow will be the same, he thinks, but maybe in a different order: the sleeping, then the waking to a pine bench and then the cans of Lite, and then more sleeping. Sometimes, when he dozes, he has the sensation that he's falling off the bench to the dank concrete below, but when he wakes, he's still balanced, his spine centered in the middle of it. The spray-painted black plywood of the dugout is his enclosure, his protection, his little life.

Splintered, and smooth at the same time. The café booth was smooth and warm, too, when he slid into it and close to her.

He knows no one will disturb him here. The season for the local high school and amateur teams is over, and this ball field, in late September, is usually abandoned. Only occasional players stroll onto the field—lone, slender young men with aluminum bats on their shoulders. Sometimes they walk onto the field and disturb his peace, hitting baseballs toward the whitewashed fence in the outfield for an hour until they finally jog back to their cars, where their girlfriends, sitting on the fender and watching them, wait for them.

He tries not to think about the old days, about where he's been, because that might change where he is now. He tries not to think about it, but sometimes these slender men who come to the field make him think about it. The crack of the bat, as the man tosses a ball into the air and hits it, makes him think about the times he loped across the outfield to get beneath a high fly ball, how much time he always seemed to have. There are no watches on a baseball field, no scoreboard time clock, and games can go on endlessly, so there's no need for keeping time. He always had so much time to lunge out of his position in left, lope to his right or left, and get to a fly ball. They seemed to wait for him to glide under them with his hungry leather glove. Even the hard-hit balls to deep center seemed to hang there an extra second so he could race beneath them, reach up and hear the sound of their surprised *smack* as they landed in the webbing of his glove.

His ball games back in high school were like that—there was always just enough time, and not enough of it. Days seemed to pass by and then break apart like a fragile object. Like a glass of water in a slow motion video, falling from a tabletop to the hardwood floor. That's the way that glass looked the last time he saw her when they ordered a breakfast of pancakes at Flick's Café. That morning, she slid from the café booth bumping the glass with her thin, pale elbow. He didn't realize it at that moment, but that motion of sliding out was her way of saying goodbye. He tried to catch the glass as it fell toward the floor, but he couldn't quite reach it. It made a slight blur as it fell. Then it shattered suddenly, at their feet. "Oh," she exhaled, "Sorry. Sorry." And, as he stared at the pieces, he just echoed the word back to her. "Yeah. Sorry." Love and marriage and children: sharp shards of cloudy glass.

Now he's falling from the pine bench and landing somewhere in that Standard Oil & Tire back lot, where, after high school, he's picking up some old tires. He rolled them from the garage toward the back pile, watching them spin. Sometimes he closed his eyes as he rolled them, feeling, beneath his fingertips, their treads worn to smoothness, sensing all the miles the tires must have traveled. Worn tires were a good thing, he decided back then—they spoke to him of distance, of places he might go.

Everybody in town said he was destined to go to the Major Leagues, with his fielding and batting talents. Everyone in town thought he'd get singled out and offered a contract to a minor league squad team, and then work his way quickly up from Rookie League to Class A ball to Triple-A, and then make the leap to the Major Leagues, where he'd be a star. He was the best damn ballplayer they'd ever seen—the hometown boy from Centerville would make them smile; he'd do the town proud, his face beaming on the front page of the local paper. But for some reason—a reason even he didn't understand—he didn't keep playing. For some reason, he just fell gradually away from baseball. After high school, he never joined the Centerville Champs, the local amateur team, even though the coach begged him to. "You're going places," the grinning coach told him several times, "And fast. You know that, kid?"

But the kid didn't know that, just put his glove and bat and baseballs in a musty cardboard box in a corner of the basement and took a job at the Standard Oil and Tire station on the edge of town, where he liked rolling those tires slowly out to the back lot, where he'd feel their smoothness before he'd toss them onto the pile. Sometimes he stood there, looking up at the small, ash-gray mountain of tires, their circles upon circles upon circles, dark eyes with no pupils. He thought of all the miles and miles they're traveled, around and around the world.

"What took you so long?" his always-cranky boss, Duke Heshburger, asked him when he walked back into the garage after a tire run.

"Huh?" he'd reply, as if waking.

"What took you so damn long with those tires? I got a car here needs the oil changed."

He shrugged. In his mind he wasn't sure just how long it took to roll four tires out to the pile; each tire seemed to travel a thousand miles beneath his palm.

Heshburger pointed at him, the grease-smudged red and blue *Standard* patch rising and falling on his chest. "Keep this up and you won't have a goddamn job here. I'll fire your sorry ass."

The previous months, he had bounced from job to job around town—delivering for a lumber company, working at the implement yard with the enameled skeletons of farm equipment, standing in the aisle of a hardware store where he sorted bolts and nuts and twelve-pound nails in bins. That last one bored him to death, the nails making his palms raw, making his brain feel like it was rusting.

"Lonnie, how come you quit that job after just a couple of months?" she asked that day in the café. She leaned forward on her elbows, twirling a strand of reddish hair with her index finger. She looked at him tenderly, empathetically, as if she wanted to caress his face with her hand.

"Dunno. Just did," he replied nonchalantly. He knew it was the wrong thing to say, because he saw her lips dip into a frown. He didn't explain it any further, just lowered his gaze to the syrup, oozing off the side of his stack of pancakes.

That year when she slid out of the booth for the last time and the glass fell to the hard floor and she walked away, he moved job to job, hating each one, not sure how long he'd stayed at the last one, so he couldn't really put an answer in that blank when he filled out the next application.

Time was like that to him. Time was the smooth feeling beneath his palm as he rolled those tires to the back lot, tires he finally set fire to, the night after ol' Heshburger fired him from his job at the station. The station was closed and dark, and he remembers the cool feeling of the rim of the beer cans on his lips, the metallic taste. There was the soft hum of the blue neon tubes around the station's picture window as he walked behind the concrete block building with his Bic lighter. He remembers how loud the *click* sounded when he bent down toward some scrap wood beneath a tire, its surface shredded from a blowout, a rusted nail poking right through its center. Then fire grew steadily, and he felt it inside his chest as he watched it flare. Everything was fast and slow. He turned and ran from the lot, his shoes hushing in the cinders of the alley in slow motion.

Later, when the squad car pulled over and the sheriff questioned him, he could see the flames from the station rising into the sky behind, the orange glow reflecting in the picture windows on all the houses of this town. "So where you running this time of night?" the cop asked.

"What time of night?" he remembers answering flippantly, still holding that lighter in his hand.

The judge sent him up for six months in the county workhouse, and then he hitched out to Montana for a couple of years, and by the time he returned to Centerville, bearded and heavier and wearing sunglasses, he didn't know who he was. His mother and father had both passed away, and the old house was sold off by some distant relatives he hardly knew. The kid who was the baseball sensation felt like an ordinary piece of scrap paper, scuttling across the sidewalk in the wind. Not just scrap paper—he was more like a piece of transparent Saran Wrap; the people in town–even his former coach—didn't recognize him. They always seemed to be looking right through him to something else.

One day he saw the woman he once loved on the sidewalk. Headed toward the train depot, she pushed a red stroller with a little child inside. The man walking next to her held a suitcase in one hand while his other arm curved around the small of her back. As he passed the three of them, she looked at him and tipped her face to the side, as if there was something familiar about him. She gave him a nod and a slight smile as if she was being polite to a stranger, then shifted her eyes ahead again. He spun around toward her as she continued to walk. "Sorry," he wanted to call out to her. But he couldn't. His vocal chords felt like broken glass.

The longer he stayed in Centerville, the more transparent he got. Eventually he could see right through his own wool coat, a coat that once kept him warm.

"Move along. Move along, now," a cop would say to him when he'd spot him slouched in the café doorway. "You can't sleep here, buddy. We got a shelter in town."

"What time of night?" he'd mumble.

Today he jolts awake from a short doze and opens his eyes and it's not night at all; it's late afternoon. The low sun skims the shingles of the houses in the neighborhoods beyond the black left field scoreboard, lined with all those white zeros. He's riding the smooth, rough pine board toward something. As always, it's moving and not moving. As always, it's taking him toward the next day, taking him somewhere and nowhere at the same time. But what better place to ride it than in a dugout, he asks himself, where no one bothers him? A dugout with the September outfield gradually turning brown and bristly, and the sound of the locomotive's wheels moaning out their rusty song on the tracks. Down Main Street, he can almost hear the red cushion of a café booth sighing as a couple slides from it.

He doesn't want to think about the baseball days, though sometimes they come back to him—the way he slid like melted butter across the field when he was a slender ballplayer. The way he hit a high fly ball once, and, on its descent, it almost hit a blackbird that swooped in the sky. The two of them—leather ball and feathered bird—almost colliding a hundred feet in the air. But they never touched.

Now he sits up, lifts his legs, lets them fall toward the concrete floor of the dugout. They drop slowly, as if in a grainy slow-motion video. He sees the glass falling again, thinks about that woman, walking out, him still sitting there, the pooled pancake syrup slowly hardening.

He stands in his dark brown boots, straightens his body, his spine creaking like the call of a distant bird. He's tired, but he's awake, too. A few blackbirds glide over center field and he stares at them for a long time. The birds circle, and circle, and circle on themselves, carving a hole in the blue sky. He feels himself carving a hole in the air where he stands, he parts a little space, and that's who he is. It's the most and least he can be.

His legs feel numb, but still, he leans forward and takes a step. One step, then another, wobbly, almost, like he's a small child learning to walk. He feels like he could almost break into a run, but he doesn't. Instead, he shuffles toward the batter's box and the golden sand that surrounds it. He reaches down to home plate and rubs his palm across it. Its surface is concave; it's smooth, but a little rough, too, from all the cleats gouging into it for years. He thinks for a moment about breaking into a run around the bases, just for the joy of it. But he doesn't. He pictures himself sprinting all the way around, and then, finally, dropping into a climactic slide into home plate. Or maybe he'd dive head-first, daring, and safe. But he doesn't do that either. His boots are heavy; his feet feel like they're stuck in something.

Best to stay where he is, he tells himself. Best to just let that image of her sliding out of the red vinyl booth stay back there in the past, like a mirage that's about to fade if you get too close. Just forget it, and forget the blank look on her face when she saw him on the street. Let all those memories stay hardened in that amber syrup. Just stand here and tip your head back, he tells himself. Feel the early evening breeze that climbs to its feet and rushes across the field.

Then he notices a small whirlwind of dust, swirling up on the infield. He watches as it rises higher, the rotating brown dirt lifting ten feet in the air. The dust devil pulls the sound of the train whistle inside it, spinning it around and around. He recalls that some Native tribes believed dust devils were a sign of someone's spirit, rising to greet you. As the whirlwind gets closer, he doesn't close his eyes to the stinging dust. He just feels it— rough, yet smooth, as it pauses, caresses his face, and then drifts past him.

REAL BALLPLAYERS WEAR THE CHAPSTICK THEIR WIVES GAVE THEM

Before I leave the house for a game, my wife pulls something from a Walgreen's bag and holds it in front of me. It's a thin tube of ChapStick.

"It's got sunscreen in it," she says, almost apologetically.

I feel myself cringe and ask, "It's not a Revlon, is it?"

"Of course not," she assures me, "it's Panama Jack."

"Oh?" I reply, not really knowing exactly what she's getting at.

"It's a fifteen. Thought you could use it," she says, brushing her hair back from her face. Her hair is smooth, like a blonde wave from the sea. "You know—when you're standing in the sun in the outfield."

"Yeah," I say, with my patented shrug. I love her for her concern, for thinking about my welfare on the field. Love her for wanting to protect my lips. After all, as a veteran player in the over-35 league, I need all the help I can get with the screaming line drives coming at me and the taste of the harsh, afternoon July sun.

"You can keep it in that zipper pouch in your duffle bag," she offers. "That way, the guys don't have to see it."

"Sure. Sure. I will." I appreciate the way she gives me an option, a way to save my dignity and to seem macho—yet still protected—on the ball field. She knows that if some of my burly teammates saw the fluorescent orange tube of SPF 15 lip balm in my duffle, rolling around like some girly makeup, they might razz me, saying "Dude, what's that? Lip gloss? What are ya here for—a ball game, or fashion photo shoot?"

The thing about baseball wives is that they sometimes have a different agenda than their husbands. For instance, her main farewell when I leave for a game is not "Have a great game," or "Good luck," or "Get some hits tonight," but instead, "Don't try to be a hero and get hurt out there."

Getting injured is the last thing a ballplayer thinks about as he dons a jersey for a game. Granted, I've had my share of late-inning injuries. A huge strawberry slide wound on my calf; I couldn't wear long pants for three weeks. Two pulled hamstrings—one that blossomed into a soft-ball-sized blue bruise on the inside joint of my right knee—causing me to limp around the house for months. Bruised ribs from slamming into the outfield fence; I was certain they were broken, but an X-ray assured me they were still whole. Then there was that torn rotator cuff. It wasn't due to inspiring the crowd by pitching a ball at 90 miles an hour, but rather from my attempt to stretch a double into a triple. When a third baseman, who, crouching low, waited to tag me on a throw from left field, I leaped into a high dive over the top of him.

That dive looked pretty good from a distance, one teammate remarked. But I was out, of course.

As the seasons pass, when I take the field for a game, my attitude has changed since my early playing days. The main thing I think about now is not making a great play, or knocking in the winning runs, or stealing bases. It's about not embarrassing myself. It's that simple: I don't want to be humiliated out there. I want to blend in, so to speak, to maintain a kind of status-quo of ballplayers, which involves competent fielding, steady base running, and consistent, reliable batting. In other words, I want my performance to hover a little above average: not dropping a fly ball, nor getting thrown out at second, nor striking out with the bases loaded.

Her priorities are different, and I know it's because she cares. Her thoughts are less about psychological humiliation, and more about physical well-being. Once, as I headed for a game, she called out "Don't break a leg or anything." That sentence caused me to freeze in the doorway. Unnerved, and not ever considering that possibility, I looked down at my legs.

Deep down, I know her warnings are important, and very real. I know she cautioned about the broken leg because she wanted me to keep playing, to not be hampered by any nagging injuries, to not let some accident keep me from the game I love. Besides that, she also wanted me to be in good condition for that vacation we had planned in two weeks. A cast on my leg would—undoubtedly—ruin a jog on the beaches of California or a snorkel trip on a bay in Hawaii.

When I return from the game, grass stained and winded, I shoulder through the front door, and slip off my muddy spikes off in the entryway. "How'd it go?" she asks from the couch, a late show flickering on the TV.

"Fine. Went one for three," I say, lifting off my ball cap from my sweat-matted hair. The cap has a series of salt rings on the inside—one for every game, like the rings on a tree. "Didn't drop any. And we won."

"No 911 calls?"

"No injuries." I affirm, walking toward her in my socks to show her that both legs and ankles are intact, and that my right arm is still happily attached to my shoulder. "And...," she inquires tentatively, "did you use that ChapStick I gave you?"

"Yup," I reply.

"Oh." Then, sounding startled, she exhales the word again, as if she really didn't expect me to try it. "Oh."

When she gives me a doubting look, I add some details: "It worked, I guess. Anyway, it tasted fine. Sort of a vanilla flavor, right?"

"Are you *sure* you used it?" I can tell she thinks I might be bluffing, and that I left the small tube wallowing among the sunflower seed shells at the base of my canvas bag. "Positive." I stare at her lips for a few seconds, pink and shapely as they curve around her words. And, like an outfielder about to dash in to make a dazzling catch, I lean forward toward them for a kiss, just to prove it to her.

THE UNLIKELY ONES

Deep down, they know they don't have to be this way. Deep down, they know that something inside them could rise, and take flight, almost, though it never does. Matt Spriggs has learned to understand that. And his girlfriend Jenelle is beginning to wonder about it.

He's one of the unlikely ones, the ones who tried out for baseball because they enjoyed the game, but they really weren't right for any position: they couldn't throw a speedball like some kids. They couldn't dash across the outfield to catch a looping liner. They weren't quick enough to lunge to their left or right at shortstop, stabbing a bounding grounder. And they weren't tall enough to become first basemen, their arms and legs too stocky to snag the sky. No, they couldn't be any of these things; they couldn't possibly be graceful or quick. But they were solid, and wide behind home plate, and reliable, so they became what they were meant to be: a catcher.

A catcher. That's what Matt Spriggs has always been, from his first little league game until today, playing for an amateur league team at age 32. Catcher: the blocker of skipping low pitches, the stopper of foul tips with the glove or chest protector or bare blue thumb, or worse, the crotch. Catcher: a crouched crustacean with those heavy orange and black shin guards, the man imprisoned behind the bars of the mask, a mask blocking his vision from the rest of the world.

Catch the ball. Catch the damn ball. That's the only objective, Matt tells himself when he squats behind home plate before each game. He'll never make it to the big leagues, or even the minors, and he knows that. He'll never be a Mike Piazza or Sandy Alomar or Joe Mauer, those rare All-Star catchers who can boost their average toward .350 and hit the ball 450 feet. He knows his place. Catcher—the one position that no-body else wants on this team, and that's that.

He's the target the pitcher aims at. His job is to focus on the ball as it curves outside the plate or does a nosedive below the batter's knees or cuts inside or comes straight and true, a fast ball seeming to rise as it startles the air. No dreaming for the man behind the plate, no luxurious seconds to lope under a fly ball. Just catch the pitch. Just be steady. Just smother the ball with that big globe of leather you call a glove, swallow it each time, and then look the runner back to first to make sure he doesn't steal. Some people call it a boring, utilitarian position, but he doesn't think so. Never mind the sweat that stings your eyes on humid summer days, never mind the way you're covered in a layer of equipment, a thick, sopping-wet chest protector that seems to weigh a thousand pounds. Through all this, he's glad his girlfriend Jenelle is always there, behind him in the stands, lightening his load a little.

You'd never describe Matt Spriggs as small; weighing over 260 pounds, his thighs are like stone pillars, his chest wide as a brick wall, and able to stop his pitcher's best eighty-five-mile-an hour fast ball cold. His girlfriend Jenelle respects him for the way he plays—his endurance, his stability. "You're my boulder behind home plate," she told him as they snuggled on a blanket in the park one evening last summer. "My sweet, sweet boulder. My Rock of Gibraltar." He stared at her, never losing sight of the curves of her cheeks. For him, she's like a first long, cool drink of lemonade after the ninth inning on a hot August day.

He accepts it that he's not like the tall, lean pitchers, always in the spotlight, all eyes on them as they adjust their cap after each pitch. When Matt catches, there's nothing much to think about, except giving that signal between your knees that only the pitcher sees—one for a fast ball, two for a curve, three for slider—and then watch him wind up, wrapping his arms and legs into a pretzel. Then, somewhere in that confusion of flesh, his arm comes down and he fires the ball toward you. Nothing to think about except to open your leather mouth. Consistent: never less, never more. Dull, some people might say. Nothing to think about except the thump of the ball in the pocket, your hand stinging a little, but getting a little more used to it each time.

Lately Jenelle has been throwing probing questions at him, questions he doesn't quite know how to field. "Why do you still do it?" she asks as she crosses her legs in her faded blue jeans on the pilled beige sofa. "I mean, why do you want to be a catcher?"

"I just am, I guess," he replies, gazing idly at the new aquarium Jenelle set up in the corner of the living room, where betas and guppies swim through the silvery bubbles. The angelfish always seem to do a fluttering graceful dance around the tank. But there's one small one—a kind of odd-looking gray speckled catfish—that scuttles at the base near a ceramic castle on the layer of pebbles.

"But at your age, you could be doing other things. Instead it's four games a week. And always on Sunday, all summer long."

"What other things do you mean?"

"Maybe helping me remodel my kitchen, like we always talked about. And," she suggests, "we could go to movies on Sunday afternoons."

When he seems to shrug, she glances down at his right hand, the knuckles swollen where two of his fingers were broken. "Why put yourself through it?"

The questions are the same questions Matt has heard from her lately, and he gives his usual answer. "Because deep down, I want to," he replies. "Deep down, I like it."

"You *like* being hit with a foul tip?" Jenelle questions, a frown melting her lips. There's a suddenly harsh tone in her voice that he hasn't heard before. "You *like* heading to the clinic after a game to see if your hand is fractured or not?"

"Well, no," he replies, his thick eyebrows almost meeting in the middle. "No, not that."

Just fun to *be* there, you know? Just fun to be part of the team."

"Yeah," Jenelle adds skeptically, "the team. You're lucky if you win a couple games a season."

"So what if we're near the bottom?" Matt asks. "What's wrong with that?" He gives her a half-grin with his thick lips. "Somebody's gotta be near the bottom. Otherwise there's no top, *or* no bottom, either."

She just lets out a frustrated sigh.

When the cell phone rings, Jenelle walks to the kitchen and picks it up from the table. Matt leans close to the aquarium and peers in. He stares at the tiny catfish, resting on the layer of polished stones, its odd, oval mouth opening and closing as it inhales the water. It's camouflaged there, and its small black eyes seem to stare back at him.

Maybe that's me, he thinks as he stares at the fish. *Maybe I am a bottom feeder, like she says.*

In his recurring dream, Matt is always swimming. He's swimming somewhere underwater, and he doesn't know why. The water is silty, dark green, and murky. He can't see anything, but he keeps swimming, holding his breath, and paddling his bulky body through it.

Matt works as a night security guard at the Knight's Rest Inn. There's never much trouble in the local motel a few miles off the interstate, except for some kids occasionally dumping the trash bins out back, or throwing water balloons at each other in the carpeted hallways. Most nights at the Knight's Rest Inn are quiet, and that's the way Matt likes it. Outfitted in his white dress shirt with a bronze badge attached to it, a squawk box attached to his belt, he leans against the lobby desk and chitchats with the night clerks, then makes his rounds along the wooden runways alongside the rooms. Then he returns to the lobby occasionally for a sip of soda or coffee from the coffee maker by the TV set that's always blaring. He always takes a sandwich—Braunschweiger liver sausage on white bread, sliced down the middle—to eat as a snack. One half of the sandwich at eight o'clock, the other half at ten. Jenelle hates the stuff, says it has pork jowls and pork snouts in it, but for some reason he likes it. The Knight's Inn has a tiny indoor pool—more like a glorified whirlpool—so Matt has never been tempted to swim in it after his shift. Sometimes the front desk clerk gets a call, maybe at ten-thirty or eleven o'clock, just before his shift is over. Tonight the clerk says to the phone "I'll send security right up" and he turns to Matt. "A woman and her kids are locked out. You want to go up to 224?"

Matt saunters down the ramp to 224, shakes his head at the woman. "The old locking yourself out trick, eh?" he comments. He knows he's saying the obvious, but it'll do for the moment.

"Yeah," she says weakly, then bites her lip to show she's a little helpless. "A single mom can't keep track of her keys, I guess," she says with a light laugh. The little kids—holding stringy-haired Barbies and Super Soaker squirt guns—look up at him suspiciously, wondering who this big man is. They stare at the black and gold striped lapels on his shirt, the night stick strapped to the side of his waist.

He opens the door with his master, and the kids run in. "Thanks," she exhales. "You're too nice." She lingers for a moment in the door-way, gazing at him, smiling pleasantly.

He wonders if that look means something, but he decides it doesn't. And, because he's with Jenelle, he wouldn't act on it anyway. "You bet," he replies. Pleased that he's averted another little crisis, he pivots on his shiny black shoes and strolls the outdoor walkway toward the lobby. Halfway down, he pauses and glances at the night sky beyond the asphalt parking lot.

The stars look so clear, he thinks. It makes him feel like he's at the bottom of some great, dark sea, and all those stars are floating on the top, glittering like bits of crystal sand that never sink.

On Thursday evenings—a night when no games are scheduled—Matt likes to go down to Tubbs Bar-B-Q and Buffet. Thursday is his night out, and he drives with Jenelle in his old green Ford for the all-you-can-eat dinner. She eats a few pieces of chicken and a salad, then lowers her fork to the table. Matt will usually go back several times for more lasagna, more meat loaf and gravy, and then to the salad bar again to get another small cup of the grayish-brown pate that, to him, tastes like braunschweiger. Then, to top off the meal, he'll head to the dessert bar for some apple Betty and ice cream, topped with the non-dairy Cool Whip they keep in a large, cloudy glass bowl at the dessert bar.

"How can you possibly eat anymore?" Jenelle asked him last Thursday.

"Because I can," he replied, and he stood up and strolled to the counter to peruse the bins of bread pudding, chocolate fudge bars, and sticky Rice Krispy treats.

Lately, she keeps questioning him. And she's been talking about her uncle, who was overweight, ended up getting a double bypass, and then died from heart failure. Matt is not afraid of a heart attack, not one bit. Besides, he gets out and exercises with the team every Monday at practice and during the games every Wednesday and Sunday. Sure, he puffs and sweats during the games, but still, it's exercise.

"Doesn't eating that much make you sluggish?" she asked him when he returned to the table with a mound of fried chicken and stuffing. He slid the red paper napkin on his broad lap.

He glanced at her slim form in her tight jeans and then just gave her a quick smile.

"You never know how to answer my questions, do you?" she said, her voice suddenly a little icy, like the soft-serve swirled on top of his slice of blueberry pie.

"Nope," he said, feeling thick-skulled like a Neanderthal, "Guess I don't." He wasn't sure what she was getting at, but he knew she was talking about something besides this buffet, though.

He strolled back to the serving line. For him, eating was just something you do. It tasted good, of course, to eat that chicken with the smoky barbecue sauce on it, and the tart coleslaw, and the thick chocolate fudge on top of a brownie, but still, it was just something you did. After all, it fueled you. One of his few memories of his father— who died when Matt was a small boy, was the way he always fixed a big breakfast of pancakes and sausage and bacon, and then enjoyed a hot dog or an ice cream cone between meals. Then there was the roast beef, mashed potatoes and gravy dinner served by his mother in the evenings. It was always delicious. It's what you did.

That Thursday, after the buffet, he dreamt he was swimming again. In the dream, he felt heavy, though, so he could hardly move through the water. He seemed to be contained in a small pool, its aqua sides closing in on him, and he could see that he was displacing the water, which was splashing over on the perimeter of the pool. In the dream, he didn't know if he was swimming on the surface, or halfway down, or maybe near the bottom.

Sometimes Matt has the vague sensation that he doesn't know exactly where he is, or where he belongs. And when he starts to question himself, he snaps back and thinks, *No, I'm who I am. I'm steady. I'm right here, where I belong.*

"Ever think about seeing other people?" Jenelle asked him last weekend. She uttered the words idly as she stood in the yard behind her apartment, hanging a sheet on the line. As she stretched for the clothes pins, he could see how lean she was: the firm back of her thighs in those créme shorts, the supple length of her arms. His shadow on the lawn seemed to be double the size of hers.

"People?" he asked. "Like who?"

"I don't know," she said, a slight breeze making her straight long brown hair rise and fall.

"Just other people."

"Um, no," he said. "Why?"

"Ever just *think* about it?"

"Not really."

"Why not?"

"Because I'm with *you*," he replied. He realized when he said it that it wasn't much of a reply, but it was as deep of an answer as he could muster at that moment. Then a sheet filled with air and billowed against his face and body, blocking him from Jenelle. He realized, at that moment, that everything she said lately about one thing was really about something else.

Inside, while Jenelle was in the kitchen talking on the cell phone with a girlfriend, he stared at the glowing light reflecting off the aquarium, the silvery bubbles from the aerator rising, one by one, to the surface. The bigger fish sometimes eat the smaller fish, Jenelle once told him. It's nature, she said, it's what they do. Matt studied that black and gray speckled catfish at the bottom with its whiskered face, the way it slid on its belly over the rounded pebbles at the base of the tank, then paused for long minutes without moving, camouflaged.

At the game the next Sunday, Matt bends on his haunches and catches the full nine innings. Someone once joked with him that catchers are dumb because they sit on their haunches so long that it cuts off the circulation to their brains. He knows for sure that when he stands up quickly after a long inning, he feels a little dizzy, the blood rushing to his head.

Today the opposing team has three or four small, wiry guys who like to try to steal second on Matt, and he hates that. He hates it that he's sluggish this afternoon, and short of breath. Throwing the baseball to second is like heaving a heavy rock. The ball seems to travel only halfway there, then skips a couple of times before it reaches the second baseman's glove, always after the runner's foot slides safely into the bag. That play opens up a two-out rally for the other team, and they score five runs. Coach Phillips, a chunky man in his late fifties with a shape like a wrecking ball, gnaws on a splintered toothpick and scowls at Matt between innings. Matt knows Phillips would replace him if he could, but there's no other catcher on the team. By the time the game's over, the opposing players steal four or five bases on Matt, and his team loses by a dozen runs.

It doesn't matter if I throw these guys out or not, he tells himself, justifying his bad game. He shifts his weight on the varnished pine plank in the dugout, picks up a batting helmet and squints at it as if there's something of importance there, some meaningful hieroglyph in the foam padding and dust. *We weren't destined to win today anyway,* he thinks. *But maybe next week I'll throw somebody out. Maybe next week I'll have a good game. I'm a backstop, as the coach once called me. I'm grounded. I'm Matt Spriggs, the team anchor.*

After the game, he drives through town in his Ford, glancing at the old frame houses of the neighborhood that seem to lean their weight against the pillars of their front porches. He stops at Jenelle's apartment, but she's not there. Just a note on the door that reads:

"Matt—Had to go someplace after the game.
Might be back late tonight. See you tomorrow?"

He has nothing better to do, so he decides he'll sit and wait for her. He lowers himself to the cool concrete of the front step for a while. *Maybe she's out with her girlfriends,* he thinks, *but that's not likely, not on a Sunday night.* He'll wait for her for as long as it takes. He sits there a half hour, staring at the oak trees in the yard, their crisscrossed branches above him, and, beyond them, the stars. His mind wanders. He thinks about rising up to that surface of the stars someday, and what it might be like. He closes his eyes, and dreams a little about it. He sees them shimmer, then pull away from him.

An hour later, he opens Jenelle's front door with the master key he uses at work, and steps into her dark apartment. Inside, the only light is the glow of a small bulb at the top of the aquarium in the living room, and, drawn to it, he walks over. He stares at that small catfish, lying motionless on the pebbles. He thinks about what it's like to be at the bottom of the tank all day, like that fish, a line of tiny, glistening bubbles from the aerator rising next to it and bursting on the surface.

He thinks about that primitive little fish, the way it scuttles along the base of the tank on its belly. He thinks about how, someday, it might evolve and sprout nubs from the sides of its body. It's against the odds, but he considers that those nubs could evolve and grow into four legs, and that one day, to everyone's amazement, that fish would swim upward, would rise from deep down on the bottom to the surface and crawl up on dry land, its gills absorbed, its tiny chest cavity expanding with delicate lungs. He's heard about such things on the *National Geographic* channel. How amazing it would be to be sitting on a rock somewhere near a lake, and to actually *see* that evolution happening—to see that water creature crawl, shivering, onto dry land for the first time. It *did* happen, a couple million years ago, and he wonders if anyone—one lone, hunched, near-human—might have been there to witness it.

He wonders, if he waits long enough by this glass tank, that maybe he'll be the one to see that happen. Maybe he'll be the person who sees the fish rise, steadily rise to the surface, and then crawl onto the side of the glass, to see that fish becoming more than it ever was, more than anyone ever thought it could be.

It would be really amazing, he thinks. It's unlikely, but it could happen. But for now, he'll wait.

Before he knows it, it's already one o'clock in the morning. *Patience*, he tells himself, and he lowers himself to the beige sofa. *Steady. Just wait.*

Soon it's two a.m.. Then three.

Jenelle never stays out this late; when she's out with the girls, they're always back by ten-thirty or eleven. He's beginning to realize that maybe he's missed some signals, and it's a little hard to judge where the ball might be going to break. He strolls to the fish tank again, crouches down next to it and stares into it, his eyes puffy from the dust of tonight's game.

At that moment he hears a click as a key slides into the door. It's Jenelle, laughing lightly. There's a voice behind her: it's a man's voice, saying goodbye to her. The sound of that voice thumps Matt hard in the chest like being hit by a fast ball when you're not wearing a chest protector. The man leaves. She walks into the room, about to flip on the lights, and sees Matt. Still crouching, he slowly pivots toward her.

"Matt? Is that you?" she calls, surprised. "What are you doing here?"

The air suddenly seems thick as he stands up, the blood rushing to his head making him dizzy. He feels something from deep down climbing up inside him: words, one by one. Small words, but meaningful ones. Words he hasn't yet spoken, but needs to. And he finally knows how he'll answer her.

THE BASEBALL WIFE
AT THE START OF THE SEASON

It's beautiful to watch: she's never swung at a baseball before, but when I pitch the ball to her, she swings and Monarch butterflies rise from the wooden barrel. She swings, and sunlight scatters like shards of splintered glass. Rescued from the bottom of the duffel, my old batting gloves are worn and loose on her hands, grime darkening the leather palms like storm clouds.

She swings again and the clouds vanish. Swings once more and last year's oak leaves scatter from the bat, and a Canadian goose arcs gracefully over the field, heading north again for the spring.

"Take a break," I say after a half-hour, knowing she must be tired. Just thinking about the way her arms will be sore tomorrow makes my muscles feel stiff. But she won't step out of the batter's box, crouches there like she's memorizing every scratched scar on that weathered home plate, levels the bat over it like she's leveling the horizon, waits for me to toss the next pitch. She'd stay on this diamond until evening, until it's too dark to see the ball, her hands learning the resonant song of leather and wood, wood and leather.

Later, the batting gloves, exhausted, curl in the darkness of the zipped duffel, wishing for the shape of her slim hands to slide into them again.

In the middle of the night, we lie on a wrinkled field of sheets. I'd cross a thousand chalk lines to embrace her. She reaches toward me, her soft, strong arms aching but still dreaming of just one more swing, a swing that would hit the moon squarely and shatter it to luminous pieces, doubling the stars in the night sky.

THE RABBIT IN THE BATTING CAGE

In memory of K. P.

I never was able to tell this story. I tried many times, but I couldn't quite put it into words, so I closed it into a small cardboard box in my mind and kept it to myself. But today I'll try to explain it, to convey the music and sorrow of an early spring day. Today I'll tell the story of that rabbit, caught in the batting cage.

Here's how it begins: One afternoon last April, after the winter snows had finally melted, I stopped at a sandlot field outside of town to hit a few baseballs with my six-year-old son. Pulling my duffle and Louisville Slugger from the trunk of the car, I tipped my head back and inhaled the early spring air; it tasted sweet, like tentative green tendrils, sprouting from the ground. Overhead, a layer of clouds unfolded to display the amber gem of the afternoon sun. The wavering layers of heat began to rise, tentatively, for the first time in months from the moist, sandy infield.

We walked toward the small field, my six-year-old son trailing behind me, humming an unrecognizable tune. Reaching home plate, I tossed a few baseballs into the air and hit them toward the outfield fence in left. The sound of the wooden bat was just right; the stands of pine trees alongside the field tossed the echoing *crack* back and forth, back and forth. I hit about a dozen baseballs, a few of them clearing—or bounding over—the leaning wire fence in left. An old batting cage—its heavy black net strung and sagging between galvanized posts—paralleled the fence, and my last hit actually landed on top of it, sending a ripple through the rest of the net before it rolled down the slant and back to the ground.

"Nice one, Dad!" my son cried, looking up from the dandelion he'd just picked.

We jogged out to retrieve the baseballs on the inside of the fence, then stepped through a creaking gate to the other side for the rest. It was then that I noticed something at the far end of the batting cage. At first, I didn't know what the gray shape was. As I stepped closer, I realized that it was a rabbit. A dead rabbit, inside the net, caught in the thick strings. It was suspended there, vertically, a few inches off the ground, as if it had struggled and struggled to get out, climbing up the knotted net as it did. The net seemed to spiral around its decaying body, hugging it. I wondered how a rabbit got inside the batting cage, since the perimeter of the net was draped all the way to the ground and weighted down with small sandbags. Then I noticed one of my baseballs resting directly below the rabbit; it appeared as though the ball had taken a hop, struck the carcass, and then fell just inches from the rabbit's outstretched hind legs.

I didn't really want to look at the rabbit; it wasn't something I wanted to acknowledge on this idyllic April day with my son.

So I reached down, trying to keep my eyes fixed on the gray printed label on the baseball that was smeared like a cloud. But before I stood up, I couldn't help but glance at the carcass. The rabbit's pale white sockets—the place where its eyes used to be—seemed to stare at me. I quickly looked away.

A few feet from me, my son skipped across the grass as he gathered a few of the baseballs. He pulled the front of his T-shirt from his shorts and collected them in the cloth.

"Find them all, Daddy?" he asked, starting toward me.

"Don't come over here," I cautioned. He was only six, and I didn't want him to be upset by the grisly sight—the net strangling the rabbit's torso, its matted, tufted fur riffling in the breeze, the paws reaching outward as if dreaming of leaping. The eyes sunken into its skull as if it was looking inward into something dark and endless.

"What's that?" He craned his head to the side. I realized he had spotted it, and I didn't answer. During that pause, a few crows cawed in the distance, a raspy, scratching sound.

"A rabbit," I finally replied, stepping toward him. "That's all."

"Rabbit?" His voice rose a little.

"Yeah," I said, wincing. I bent to one knee, trying to block it from his view. "But it's not, it's not alive…"

With that, he pushed past me and leaned close to the carcass. "What happened to it?" he questioned. "Why is it in a batting cage?"

"It got lost, maybe," I suggested as I put my hands on his shoulders, trying to veer him away.

"Lost?"

I didn't reply at first, but wanted to say: Like a lot of things, it found its way into something, but couldn't find its way out. And for a moment I wondered how long it had to writhe there. I pictured it struggling, and the more it struggled, the more the net tightened, slowly choking it. I hoped it didn't have to suffer there for long. "Come on," I finally said, "Let's get the rest of the baseballs."

"You should cut it loose," my son said, surprising me. "We should give it a funeral."

When I shrugged, he added, "I could sing a little song for it. And then we could bury it."

What he said reminded me of what I did as a kid, years ago, with stray dead birds and squirrels we found in the neighborhood yards. My sister and brother and I would place them in shoeboxes and ceremoniously bury them in the backyard garden. There was no song, though—we just buried the creatures and sent them on their way.

"Yeah. I know what you mean..." I thought about cutting it down and putting it to rest beneath the altar of grass. But I had no knife, no way to cut the tough strings that clung to it, nor a shovel for digging. Besides, to cut those strings would create a gaping hole in that batting cage. And, I reasoned, leaving an opening in the net might make more dead. "But I don't think we can do that," I added.

"Oh," he said with a muffled sound, like someone knocked the wind out of him. "Oh."

Still, he kept staring at me as if I should do something, as if I was a magician who could wave a wand over the rabbit and bring it back to life. And I almost felt guilty that I couldn't do that. I wanted to do something miraculous for him, wanted to more than anything.

"Why did it die like that?" he asked, his voice a little more demanding, though I could sense tears welling up behind his words. "Why?"

For the next few seconds, everything seemed to be waiting for an answer: my son, the field, the rabbit. But, glancing up at the huge sky above us that suddenly looked blue and hard, I just shrugged helplessly, and kept silent. A breeze swirled across the field and when it reached us, I could hear a harsh whistling sound as it cut through the diamond shapes of the black net.

I wasn't sure how to reply to him. I thought of saying *Sometimes things just get caught in a net,* but instead I mumbled "I really don't know." I wanted him to look ahead to his future, to forget about this moment, though I could tell by the expression on his face that he might not. The thought occurred to me that the image of the strangled rabbit might surface in his nightmare that night. I hoped, instead, that he'd see the rabbit in a pleasant dream, see it freeing itself from the net and bounding away, darting left, then right, then left across the field and then disappearing into the thicket of woods.

"Did we get all the baseballs?" I asked, trying to shift his attention back to gathering them. I nodded at the cluster—nestled like leather eggs—in the basket of his T-shirt. "Count them up. We should have all nine."

He obliged, pointing to each one, though, between his counting, he seemed to glance over my shoulder toward the rabbit.

"Ready to head back?" I asked.

"But aren't you going to hit some more?" He knew I usually stayed longer at a field, hitting three or four sets for at least a half hour.

"Naw," I replied. "We should go soon." I checked my watch as though we were late. "Mom will wonder where we are."

As we pulled away, I glanced in the rear-view mirror at the batting cage, watched its shadow-gray rectangle shrinking smaller and smaller. I told myself that it was just a rabbit. Just an unfortunate rabbit. That was all. Still, for some reason I didn't understand, I was the person who was chosen to find it, the one—if I told this story well enough and carefully enough—who could somehow bring it back to life.

So I'm trying to do that now.

And here's how the story ends: On the way back that afternoon, neither of us talked like we usually did. The only sound was the monotone drone of the worn tires as we followed the asphalt road back to town. My son—his seat belt fastened in the back—tilted his head and gazed at the passing rows of trees. I hope he noticed their first buds exploding with tiny green tufts.

I turned a corner and, squinting into the low sun, drove down Oak Street toward our house. It was then that I thought I heard something.

It was my son, humming.

He hummed for a few seconds, then began to sing in the back seat, his soft voice high and sweet. I listened. I couldn't quite make out the words, and didn't recognize the tune, but I knew he was singing, and maybe that was enough. Enough for him. For me. For all three of us.

ZEN BASEBALL: WHY BALLPLAYERS ALWAYS LOOK TOWARD THE RIVER

1

When I drive past the ballfield a block from my house, I often notice ballplayers, when they've finished their game, standing at the shore of the river and staring out at the slow-moving current. Who knows what those players see out there? If they were fishermen, you might be able to guess what's going on in their minds—maybe they're envisioning that huge bass that got away one morning when they fished there, or maybe the lunker walleye they might catch next week. But why do you sometimes see a lone ballplayer—a glove on one hand—standing at the edge of the river, gazing at its opaque surface? There's no telling what they're thinking when they look at all that steadily-moving water.

2

Let me tell you something important: a river has bordered every baseball field in every town where I've lived.

The summers I was in little league in Wisconsin, we played our games on the woolen mill fields, where the outfield was bordered by the Baraboo River, a slow-rolling, deep river, its muddy waters a flat brown. That river feeds into the Wisconsin River, and the Wisconsin into the Mississippi. Ours was a mysterious river, because you could never see into its opaque surface. There was a rumor among the neighborhood kids that Old Man Prawl once reeled up a skeleton hand with his fishing rod. As the story went, the bony hand rose a few inches above the water, then it fell off the hook and dropped back in as he screamed in horror. It was probably just a stick, one neighbor kid said. But most of the kids insisted that he saw it. It was real, they claimed.

During one little league game, I hit a ball that flew over the rust-colored wood snow fence and into the river. It wasn't a long hit—perhaps only two-hundred eighty feet—but I was thrilled because it was the only time I hit one there. As the ball landed, I saw the splash—a dirty beige crown—rise and fall in the water, water which sealed over and then glided so slowly you could hardly tell if it was moving or not.

3

Sometimes, standing in the outfield, the thought occurs to me: my feet are touching the grass, and the grass touches the edge of the river, and the river reaches all the way to the sea. In a way, my toes are touching the sea.

Perhaps the beauty of all land is that it was once touched by the sea. The beauty of the sea is that it's surrounded by the shape of the land. The beauty of the earth is that it always embraces itself.

4

My hometown high school field was bordered by the Baraboo River, too, but a only a player with tremendous power could hit one that far. The river flowed past the high school track in center, at least 450 feet from home plate. I've always remembered when a big, six-foot-four first baseman named Jimmy hit a ball into the river to win the conference championship game. Rawlins was muscular, and almost twice my size, even though he was only sixteen. I was just a skinny bench-warmer, and to me, his feat was amazing. I remember watching the ball land beneath the low-hanging branches of the ancient elm trees that lined the shore. Then it bounced twice and into the river. At that moment, all of us jumped from the bench in exultation, our hands above our heads. As Jimmy rounded third and strode down the line with the winning run in the bottom of the ninth, we mobbed him at home, leaping for joy as a photographer from our local paper snapped photos—catching some of us in mid-air—for the front page. After the game was over and everyone had left the field, Jimmy, his shoulders straight and proud, his spikes with their laces tied together dangling from his hand, walked barefoot out to center and gazed a long moment at the river.

5

Today, years later, I live in Minnesota, and the ball field one block from our house is bordered by the Mississippi. I read somewhere that the entire middle of our continent was once covered by an ancient sea, a mile deep in some places. After knowing that, how could I possibly stand on a baseball field, surrounded by the rippling grass blades, and feel the same way about it?

I began to believe that's the reason so many small town baseball fields are built along rivers: to connect them back to the sea.

6

When we were kids, Jimmy Rawlins loved to fish. His uncle owned a sporting goods store in a nearby town and Jimmy always came to the baseball games with a new fishing lure stuck in the fat thumb of his glove. "This one's a jig," he'd say, instructing us on the lures, "and this is a daredevil. Imagine," he exclaimed, speaking about his Uncle's store, "all that fishing gear, and I can use it whenever I want to."

Before one game, Jimmy pulled the hook from the glove and let the shiny spoon-shaped silver and black lure twirl in the air. "I caught the biggest walleye on this lure." The way he said it flatly told me he wasn't bragging, just relating a fact. "It was at least a fifteen pounder, but when I was pulling it in, I'd swear it weighed a hundred. Fell off the hook at the last minute, though," he added.

"What happened then?" I asked.

"I scooped my hand into the water to try to snag it." He laughed. "But no luck."

7

My son is convinced that, when he was five or six, he watched me hit a baseball across the Mississippi.

"It never happened," I said with a laugh, knowing that, where we live, the river is almost a quarter-mile wide. He must have watched me one time when I hit an old ball—its cover torn off—into the water. I'd found it in a forgotten box I'd kept since high school, and one day after a workout, on an impulse, I tossed it into the air and hit it into the Mississippi.

"I could never hit one that far." I confessed to my son.

"Yes you did," he insisted, in that way young sons always want to make their fathers better than they are, "I remember. I saw you hit it. And it went all the way across the river."

8

During our first winter in Minnesota, my wife and I walked onto the ice of the Mississippi. The air was warm in the March sun, most of the snow was gone, and, feeling a spring fever impulse, we strolled out to the middle. I remember thinking how the surface was frozen, but under our feet, beneath that layer of ice, hundreds of thousands of gallons flowed each second. I realized that only a few frozen inches of this river was standing still, while the rest rushed beneath it like it always had, like it always will.

Near the middle, we crouched down on our knees, cleared a circle in the layer of snow and looked through that dark, 10-inch thick window.

Our noses close to the ice, we peered as if we had a magnifying glass and could see our futures down there. At that moment, we heard the ice shifting. It cracked somewhere near us, making a sound like distant, unexpected pistol shots. We stood up quickly and embraced for a moment in fear, and then hurried back to shore, gasping. We were later told by a friend that it was foolish to walk onto the river that late in winter, that we were tempting fate, and we were lucky we didn't fall through the ice. The powerful current would pull us under and would have drowned, they told us.

Later I thought about how strange it was that often the thinnest of things—fractions of an inch, fractions of a second— separated the fools from the heroes, the lucky from the unlucky, the winners from the losers, the living from the dead.

9

At a class reunion, I spotted Jimmy Rawlins across the room, so I strolled over to talk to him. Though he was only in his thirties, he looked paunchy in his tan business suit. Back in town, he now owned the hardware store in town—a place he inherited when his father passed away. Years had slid by us, and he told me he had joined the army and fought in one of the Middle East conflicts.

"It changes you," he sighed.

"How?" I inquired.

"It just does. Holding a rifle like that. It's life and death."

"But hey," he said, quickly shifting the subject and toasting me with his glass of gin and sour, "Here's to the years."

"Still play baseball?" I asked him.

"Naw, not anymore," he admitted.

He leaned awkwardly over the bar, clutching his drink. "How 'bout you?"

"Once in a while, with a pick-up team, or with my kid."

"But I still spend a lot of time down by the woolen mill ball field," he said.

"Really?"

"Fishing, I mean." He paused a few seconds. "You bet," he added proudly. "With the hardware store, I get any lure I want. Any time I want. Sheeze," he exclaimed, shaking his head side to side, "it's a great life."

I took a sip of my beer. "Ever think about your home run in the playoffs?" His face softened and his eyes seemed to look inward a moment as if he was replaying it, deep in his brain. "How can I forget it?" he replied. He paused, then added, "You know, I never got that ball back."

"Oh?"

"I walked out to the river to try to retrieve it. Wanted to keep it as a souvenir, you know?"

"Sure," I agreed.

"But, heck," he continued, "by the time we were done celebrating, it was long gone. Floated downstream." He chuckled. "Sometimes in a dream, I cast in a lure and hook that ball and bring it back."

10

Today, I notice a pale, thin object on a bare spot in the outfield. I pick it up. It's a tiny round shell, about the size of my fingertip. I touch its chalky white surface, serrated like miniature ripples on water. I think for a moment about lifting it to my ear to find out if I can hear the distant waves, but realize that would be futile. Instead, I slip it into my breast pocket. I take it home and hand it to my son.

"Where'd you find it?" he asks.

"At the bottom of the sea," I answer.

11

It occurs to me now that I'm one of them. I'm one of those who, after a workout on a baseball field, pause and gaze toward the river. But I know I'm not the only one. There are thousands of us, I suspect, or even more. There are ballplayers all over the world who, after their games are finished, stand near the shore and face the flowing surface of a river.

I simply accept its steady motion, and feel calm for a moment, though I don't understand why. Maybe I'm realizing that, from one moment to the next, I never look out at the same river twice. But that's all right—you can't freeze anything to stop it from changing.

Today, as I stand on the shore, I turn and notice my son and my wife, on the hillside above the field. They seem transfixed, as if they're gazing out at the river, too.

The next thing I know, the two of them walk down to me and we stand there together for a moment, hand in hand in hand. We stare at the river because we love the little whirlpools that form on its surface. We love what feeds and quenches us, and what feeds us is the river, and what feeds the river is the sky, and what feeds the sky is the ocean. Love is what feeds us.

12

No, there is no telling what a ballplayer is thinking when they gaze out at a river.

They might be contemplating the cycles: the catches and the dropped balls, the hits and the outs, the ecsatic championships and the agonizing losses. It could be they're thinking about hitting a game-winning homer that, years ago, leaped into the water. Or maybe about hitting a baseball that somehow carries hundreds of yards and all the way across the river, where it lands next to a small boy or girl on the grass on the far shore. It's not possible, of course—everyone knows a river is always farther across than it looks.

Or it could be that they're just thinking of hitting a fly ball a couple hundred feet to the center of the river, and watching it drop slowly, a surprised splash rising around it as it slaps the flat surface. They might be picturing the way that ball could float downstream for days, gliding over Old Man Prawl's skeleton hand, floating past Jimmy Rawlins, who's fishing in an anchored rowboat, past small towns with houses crouched and leaning on the shore, past meadows and parks with lovers kissing on blankets and small kids tossing pebbles that plunk into the shallows.

They could be thinking about a baseball bobbing all the way from Minnesota, through Wisconsin and Illinois and Tennessee, to the delta in New Orleans, where it would spin in slow motion, its red seams unraveling.

Finally, the ball would rush into the huge open mouth of the sea, where, suddenly, it would be lost. The oncoming waves would crash down on the ball with their salty jaws, churning it to the silty bottom.

But then it would float back up.

No matter how tattered and waterlogged it might become, it would still rise to the surface again.

Or it could be the ballplayers aren't thinking about any of those things. It could be they're not pondering complicated journeys, but thinking about simpler things, things closer to home. Like how, on the surface, the river barely seems to move, though they know the current must be strong and steady.

And, they'll tell you, the more you try to stop it from flowing, the more it will flow. If you don't believe them, they'll tell you to try bending to one knee at the edge of the shore and scooping your hand in the water.

THE MIGRATION

Something he doesn't understand tugs at his elbows, and suddenly he turns left, veering off the boulevard. It's a landscaped boulevard he usually follows every day at 5:01 p.m., a straight four-lane thoroughfare that cuts through the suburb and leads him to his two-story luxury house with an acre of land and the swimming pool in the back. But not today. Without knowing why, he pulls into a small parking lot, clicks off the ignition of his Mercedes, and, leaving the keys in the ignition, steps out in his polished Gucci loafers.

To be..., on a field. The past few weeks, these few stumbling words kept playing through his mind, twisting and looping through it like a distant yet clear melody, though he didn't understand exactly what they meant. The first time he heard them, it was in a dream. There was nothing visual in the dream, just the sound of the words.

To be..., on a field, a field.... What did it mean? He wasn't certain. He only knew that the thought—the hesitant voice—kept speaking to him lately, the words varying slightly each time, as if it was trying to get the message clear. As if it was a radio transmission from some distant place, wavering in and out, and he couldn't quite understand it.

He only knew that the words at the end of the phrase always paused, leaving their meaning unfinished. To be *what?* he wondered. To be *what* on a field?

The question kept poking at the balloon of his mind, nudging it softly at first, then sharply, as if it expected him to act. At night, asleep, he heard the words—adding a little more to themselves each time— moving toward him as if they were gliding through a long tunnel that leads to the place where horizon meets sky: *To be..., on a field of, of....*

Now, walking toward this ragged sandlot field beneath the cloudy sky, he steps across the first base line and strides toward the outfield. This place was his favorite field as a kid, a place he hasn't set foot on for thirty-some years. He pauses in the middle of the outfield, and just stands there, on this warm September afternoon, waiting impatiently as though something is about to happen: a bolt of lightning, a storm, an earthquake, a deluge. A sudden blackness, or whiteness. Instead, there's nothing. Just nothing.

Maybe that's been his problem all these years; all these years, he's been impatient, expecting things to happen to him. Impatient for a phone to ring in his business office, for a text to appear on the shiny screen of his Android. The next important email for Robert Collins, CEO. Impatient for dry envelopes to appear in the mail and confirm real estate deals. Impatient for his friends, wife to speak to him. He watched as the deep well of his bank account filled with deposits. That account made him impatient to buy the next one-million-dollar house, or maybe a one-point-five spread, and then the next.

Here in this field, the overcast sky parts and tosses down a beam of bright yellow sunlight. The grass beneath his shoes blazes up, and soon the bright circle of light expands steadily, widening all the way to the wood-framed backstop and to the angular wires of the outfield fence and beyond it, to the row of oak trees.

Looking up, he notices, directly above him, birds in a V-formation, flying north. He thinks they might be geese, but they're so high and distant that he can't hear them honking. They're so high that, as they glide toward the horizon, they slowly disappear, and he can't really follow them.

As he surveys the field, long-lost memories filter into his mind. He pictures his childhood pals: Jimmy and Steve and Mickey, the kids he played baseball with on this field. They played day after day for hours, pitching, batting, fielding, laughing. It wasn't for money that he played, it wasn't to gain possessions, or to conquer goals—it was for fun, for the love of the game.

He pictures the concrete block shed beyond the third base line. It's gone now, razed for a new housing development, but back then, it was the shed where, some days when he was alone, he used to throw a ball, practicing his fielding, bouncing the ball three hundred times an hour, a thousand times a day, tens of thousands of times a summer. He was patient then, even if the ricocheting ball was out of his reach and he missed it. That ball, bouncing off the concrete blocks, was the rhythm of his life, the rhythm that, he realizes now, he's forgotten. Not just forgotten, but lost.

He was a dreamer then. Young ballplayers are just dreamers, he knows.

Not like the world he grew into. Money, deals, buying and selling— by the time he was in his twenties, he believed that's what made the world go around. Everything about his life became either white, like an avalanche of bond paper, or else it was dark gray, like the dull computer screen before he sits down at his luxury CEO office at Assurance An- nuity, Inc. and enters his password.

Nothing's green, he thinks now. It's the green that wants back into our lives, he's beginning to think, but we won't let it in.

To be..., the words sound inside his head. *On a field of grass...*

His mind flashes back to the times, years ago, when he strolled across the grass of the city park with his wife. They would picnic there on Sunday afternoons, sitting on a blue and white checkered blanket, a bottle of Cabernet Sauvignon from Napa Valley. They would laugh and talk, their words flowing like the small stream nearby, the clear water rolling over smooth speckled rocks. Those times were good. His wife, his high school sweetheart, his love. But a few years later, things changed. They began to argue, and the strolls through the park became less frequent. "Busy," he said, barricading himself in the opulent oak paneled study while she sat in a wicker chair on the second-floor deck in her floppy hat, staring out at nothing.

Then there was the day she left him. *Workaholic,* she accused. *Never time for us anymore.* Then she walked out the door, slammed it. The sound echoed throughout the rooms of their sprawling house in the suburbs. But then the rooms filled with a vacuous silence. That day was like a broken window, one you couldn't replace.

Since then, he let the business world come at him quickly with legers and work orders and expresso shots and beeping I-phones and in-boxes packed to bursting and hard drives bloating. It came at him in market stats and growth investments and rising and falling sirens and paper cuts on the tip of his index finger. Everything seemed to be black and white: he sat at his desk for hours and shuffled stacks and stacks of white papers, papers that mushroomed, filling the room like snow- drifts until he gasped for breath. He followed rows of black numbers marched across the screen, and behind them, all that endless whiteness. In that ever-narrowing office, his Charvet tie tugged at his neck, and he tugged at his tie as he computed the variable rates. The payouts. The structured settlements. The unrealized profits. The futures.

Abstractions, he thinks now. Every one of them is an abstraction. Nothing tangible, nothing you could ever hold in the palm of your hand.

His business world is thriving, but lately the rest of the world has been coming at him. He sees that world on the Internet, in the papers, on the nightly news: the faces of poor and hungry kids, refugees sorting through the crumbling ruins of war, the pandemics, the cemeteries, the moments of silence.

Lately the world keeps rushing toward him and he doesn't know how to process it. It's too huge, too complicated to even attempt to do something about, he often rationalized. This morning, he reached for his coffee for the next stack of folders and bumped the cup. He stared at it a long time: the white cuff of his shirt absorbing the spilled coffee as if it were dying of thirst.

But now, standing in the middle of the outfield, his thirst somehow feels quenched. He drinks in the openness of the sandlot—grass that stretches to the line of oak trees, then seems to pause there a moment, and then goes on. It occurs to him that, in his office, the black numbers will surround you; they'll grow like black holes and pull you in.

He tugs at his tie again. But this time he's untying it and dropping it to the ground where it lies like a silk snake flattened by a tire. He slips off his gray suit jacket, tosses it into the air, watches it ripple to the ground like the flag of a surrendered country.

Then he kneels down in center in his dress slacks. He can feel the blades of grass, even through the expensive Armani wool. He can feel the eyes watching him from the edge of the field, small eyes of the eight boys watching him from the faded chalk lines. The next thing he knows, they're running onto the field toward him as if to cheer him, or help him.

To be young, the voice says, finally adding more words in his head. *To be young, on a field of green, with...*

He feels himself lowering to his side on the welcoming grass that buoys him up like a calm ocean. Clutching his knees, he curls up. It's as if there's an umbilical cord reaching from the heart of the field to his stomach, nourishing him.

He lets his eyes slowly close.

When he opens them, he's in a white-walled hospital room. He can feel the wrinkles burrowing into his skin. He lies beneath taut dry sheets; it feels like he's been lying beneath them for months.

Tubes reach to his body, giving him sustenance. He's connected to a machine—a beeping machine that monitors him, second by second, as if it could stave off the future.

Children surround him. *Are they the children he and his wife always talked about?* he wonders. *The children they didn't have time for?* Whoever they are, they nod, their eyes sad and sorrowful, as if they're on the verge of weeping.

He glances down at his bed and notices that his white sheet is beginning to turn green at the edges. The greenness expands, moves from his toes, up to his knees, to his chest and neck. All that greenness ignites around him, filling the room, filling him, a greenness that's so intense that he just has to close his eyes.

When he opens them again, he's still lying on the sandlot field. He looks up to see his buddies from childhood surrounding him, all eight of them. It occurs to him that the boys should look much older. He's forty-nine, so they should be nearly that age by now, but they're not; their faces are as polished and smooth as they were when they were just nine-year-olds. "Nice catch, Bobby," he hears one of them say. It's Timmy, his best childhood friend, a person he's been out of touch with for decades. "But you really wiped out after you caught it. You okay?"

He wants to blurt out *Yeah. Not hurt at all.* But it feels like the wind is knocked out of him. There's no air in his lungs, and he can't exhale a single word.

No one says anything else to him; they just stare at him, as if waiting for something to happen.

Finally Timmy is distracted by something. He tips his head up, then lifts his arm and points to the sky.

It's then that Robert hears the distant honking sound and notices a group of geese approaching. He rises to his knees. It's an entire flock, migrating north in the spring after a long winter. One by one, the boys tilt their faces upward.

So he stands, tips his head back, too, and watches the geese, flying low, just above the tree tops. Geese, gliding closer and closer to them in a large but perfect and symmetrical V. It occurs to him that migrating geese like these must have flown over him dozens of times when the seasons changed, but, driving his Mercedes beneath them, he never looked up. He never noticed, or paid any attention.

But now he does. *To be young, on a field of green, with geese.* The words reverberate in his head. Yes, he thinks, *To be young, on a field of green, with geese migrating above it.*

The mysterious words finally fill out the whole sentence; they finally make sense. He thinks he says them aloud.

The geese stop honking and pass directly overhead, just a few feet above him. He listens intently to the subtle rush of air beneath their large, graceful wings. It's a sound like a long and soothing sigh.

And this time, as they glide beyond the field and toward the horizon, he can't help but smile as he follows their flight. He follows them. Yes, how easily he follows them.

PART FOUR:
THE DIAMOND-SHAPED
CIRCLE

JUST ONE MAGIC SWING

Charlie has dreamt about it, sure. One big, smooth swing, the ball rising from his bat toward deep left like a small planet arcing through the atmosphere and into orbit. Then he'd watch the steady, slow-motion descent as it falls far beyond the fence. He's dreamt about that ball, thumping against the blue seats of the bleachers or, better yet, slapping into the bare palm of a fan out there, who holds the ball high like some precious jewel he's just found. Then he'd round the bases triumphantly and see Coach Cy, his hero—with one foot on the dugout step—nod in approval.

He's dreamt about it, sure, because it's never happened. The moment just before he wakes, he sees that ball—as if pulled by some invisible string or quirk of gravity—reversing itself. It rises from the outstretched hands of the fans in the bleachers, spins over the field and traces an arc all the way back to his bat. As his swing reverses, he sees the ball pop in the catcher's mitt and hears the umpire bellow out *Strike Three!*

The moment he wakes, the realization comes back to him; Charlie Phalen has never hit a home run in his career with the minor leagues, not in almost 14 years. Not during all his at-bats in Class A ball, or in AA, where he's been stalled for the last few years.

He blinks his eyelids; it feels like there's a tiny coating of dust on them that takes a few seconds to clear. He sits up in bed and suddenly everything's real to Charlie again: his ring-stained wooden desk with the black cell phone balanced on one corner, the cracks in the plaster wall, branching like a map to somewhere, the off-center windows with the brown blinds he never wants to raise, or the morning light might sting his eyes. He knows he's never felt that sweet swing, that thrill the power hitters must experience when they hit the ball just right so it makes that deep-gut resonant sound, and the ball rockets high and far. He's never seen his teammates on the bench, being pulled to their feet in awe as they watch the sphere of leather fly, tracing the shape of a rainbow from the batter's box to the distant seats.

This morning he glances at his girlfriend, Alicia, still asleep next to him, the dark covers rising, falling—a sensuous, steadily moving landscape. What would she say about the dream? Seeing his flushed, panicked face, she'd probably say her usual things to calm him down: "Just a dream, Charlie. Just a dream. Keep it in perspective." Then she'd kiss his damp forehead.

Then he thinks about what Coach Cyrus would say. Coach Cy is his mentor, his advisor, the best coach he ever had during his year on the freshman team in high school. And now—by some great coincidence—Cy was the coach of this minor league team, so Charlie gets to hear his wise, Zen-like advice. "Just one magic swing is all you need, kid," Cy would say with a nod. "One magic swing. Dreams can be real, you know."

Charlie often wonders what that would feel like, how that one swing would resonate in the bones of his arms. Sometimes he muses about what he would do if he ever *did* see one of his hits flying that amazing distance over the 350 sign in left field. Would he sprint, full speed, around the bases? Would he round the bases steadily but gracefully, savoring each step between the canvas bags like the slowest runner in the world? Or would he not leave the batter's box, just stand there in awe and disbelief for a few seconds, watching the rise and fall of the white sphere, until the ump goads: "Get going, kid. It's outta here."

Alicia can tell, by the look on his face, when he's thinking about all those things. "You're dreaming again, aren't you?" she says, bringing him back. "You're always dreaming lately."

"And why shouldn't I?" he responds. "People have to dream, don't they?"

She never really has a comeback for that. She usually just raises her eyebrows for a moment, then maybe turns to arrange the purple lilacs in a vase on the dining room table.

At the game that evening, Charlie hops over the chalk line on his way to and from his position at second base. He's been stepping over the chalk line—a ritualistic superstition—for twenty years now, ever since he was on the junior high team. He's done it for so long that he's almost forgotten why he does it. Luck, maybe. Or a decent outing. Whatever—when he approaches the dugout, he glances down, gives a quick jump in his black cleats, making sure he doesn't touch the base line.

After the game, Charlie lingers in the dugout, watching the grounds crew person, laying down chalk lines on the first and third base lines for tomorrow's game. The man ties an orange string to two stakes between home plate and the outfield foul line, then pushes a small metal box on creaking wheels and follows that string. Below the cart, the white powder slides out in a steady stream, painting a line on the earth's back.

For a moment, he wonders what would happen if he *did* step on that chalk line someday—by accident or on purpose. He's thought about the consequences: would he strike out the next time at bat? Or worse: would he have a car wreck on the way to Alicia's apartment? Would he fall, writhing on the outfield grass, feeling a heart attack, like glass cracking, on the inside of his chest?

Or, he thinks, maybe nothing at all would happen. Maybe his size 14 cleat would just flop down on that chalk, and there'd be a puff of pale dust, and things would be just the same as always, the old world just spinning like usual.

Charlie had been with Alicia, steadily, all during his minor league career. He'd been with her, steadily, all during his minor league career. Been with her ever since he first met her in their twenties. That day, after a game, he was celebrating in The Tenth Inning, a small tavern on the outskirts of town. He set down his beer glass, turned, and saw her face, a rose petal, softened by the smoky haze. He strolled over, and he and Alicia talked and laughed for an hour. She drank one of those tropical drinks—flavored with coconut or pineapple juice—with a small pink umbrella in it. She left before the bar closed with her girlfriends, but as she passed him, she dropped that umbrella into his glass of beer with a coy smile. He remembers holding that umbrella up to the ceiling light, like some crazy ballplayer expecting to be protected from the rain. Then he noticed her phone number, written on the underside of it.

But now, years later, Charlie can't help the feeling that she's getting tired of him, tired of his schedule, his long road trips to humdrum towns like Wichita or Davenport, his mundane day-to-day warm-up routines. He has the feeling that she'd been with him so long now that something was about to change. She'd been reading travel magazines, and he's noticed them, on a table, purposely left open to romantic places like Tahiti or Aruba or St. Lucia.

"Everything that goes up, must come down. It's a rule of the universe." That's what Coach Cy always said, and Charlie, after his years in baseball, is starting to understand how true his sayings turn out to be. "Everything evens out. You lose one thing, but you find another." Charlie understands:

if you try to hit a bunch of home runs, you're bound to strike out a lot. Your team is hot—on a ten-game winning streak—and then they drop the next five. You find somebody's wallet and return it to lost and found at the concession stand, and then you leave your duffel behind in a faraway town's dugout.

That damn Coach Cy, Charlie thinks, shaking his head in awe, *He always comes up with a great batch of truisms.* Charlie has paid close attention to them over the years, memorized them, pondered them almost every day during his pregame warm-ups. Everything, to Cy, was a leveling process. Everything rose and then fell, everything got built up, like a mountain, and then wore down, eventually, with erosion. If it was bright and sunny one week, you'd pay for it with rain and cold the next. Cy had the whole world's philosophy in the palm of his hand, and Charlie admired him for that. But the downside was that you could never get a straight answer from the guy. "We're gonna win tonight, right, coach?" some of the younger players asked him. "Maybe we will, maybe we won't," he replied, seeming to be more interested in the gray post of the foul pole than their faces. "Sometimes you do, sometimes you don't. Only the baseball gods know for sure."

Coach Cy had the record to prove that he knew what he was doing: his lifetime wins and losses record was almost even, with 245 wins, 244 losses.

Everything *did* balance out for him.

It was a good way to approach life, Charlie thinks. But what about me? What about a guy who hasn't hit a home run in over 2000 at bats, the guy with the longest streak of games without a homer? My batting average is okay, but not great. So what's balancing things out for me? He wonders.

"Half the day's gone already." Alicia said one day when he'd been ignoring her, engrossed as he read a book about Hall of Fame players. He was studying the stats of the great all-time home run hitters: Aaron. Ruth. Mantle. Mays. Killebrew. "Let's do something," she offered. "Let's drive to Madison, or Minneapolis for the weekend. Or tour a state park. You've been paging through that book for hours."

"What's wrong with that? A guy has to dream, doesn't he?" He figured his standard flippant comeback would work again, the way a blind man knows where a chair or table are in his apartment and is able to avoid them. He knew his comment would irritate her, but he said it anyway.

"Charlie, I'm right here, right now. You don't even seem to notice that." With that, she walked out of the room, and Charlie just sat there, balancing the book in the palms of his hands.

Some nights Charlie dreams about chalk lines. Chalk lines, following that grounds crew man who plods down the field. Chalk lines, leading all the way to his apartment, painting Xs and Ys in his dingy kitchen, in his back yard, across his beat-up red Chevy in the driveway. Chalk lines, filling up Charlie's head until the whole inside of his skull was painted white. He wakes at three a.m., sweating, his mind rushing with thoughts, thoughts that could have been planted there by Coach Cy: *Lines let you know where you stand. The field, the fair and foul territory, your life. You know what counts and what doesn't, what's out there in the chaos beyond the pale, dusty line and what isn't. Things are clear, defined. Right?* He takes a long drink from the glass beside the bed, the water washing away his panic.

"I need to know your plans," Alicia says the next morning. It's a couple hours before Charlie has to report for the game, and Alicia slept over at Charlie's place again. They're sitting at the breakfast table: a dented box of shredded wheat and an over-ripe orange sitting in front of them.

"What plans?" Charlie asks.

"About us," she says. "I mean," she pauses, "I can't just stay here in limbo with you all the time. I need a commitment."

"Um….oh," Charlie stumbles. He reaches down, rolls the lopsided orange to its other side.

She looks at him and purses her lips, waiting for an answer. He doesn't reply for a few seconds, though he can sense the anxiousness simmering beneath her skin.

"I know you're really serious about your baseball, and I understand that," she says, standing from the table and faces the wall. "But I need to know when you're giving up this…this boy's game and getting a real career."

"It *is* a career," he responds.

"It might be," she says, spinning around. Her face flushes pink with frustration. "But *only* if you make it to the Majors, which you haven't yet," she says, her words rushing out. "And even if you did, a career only lasts until you're about thirty-five. Then it's over. Then you've got to find something else. And thirty-five's only a couple years away for you. Then what?" Her voice softens a little and then she adds, "I love you, Charlie. You know that. That's why I'm worried about you." She grabs his hand.

He pulls his hand back and says, "I know, I know. I love you, too. But I want to stay where I am right now. I like being in baseball." He stands from the table, bumping it with his thigh, and the milk from the cereal bowl spills onto the table. "No, I mean I *love* being in it."

She's silent for a few seconds, then finally exhales, "Then you might lose something." She doesn't explain what she means, and it bothers him, the way she gets that pained, distant look on her face, like a pitcher who's just given up a grand slam.

Charlie thinks a moment, then finally blurts "Easy come, easy go. That's what Coach Cy always says. Half a dozen of one, or six of the other." The moment the words slip through his lips he knows he's being being a little flippant and sarcastic, and he regrets them.

Alicia just shakes her head, her auburn hair falling over one eye, turns, grabs her key chain from the coffee table and heads to her car.

"Where you going?" he calls to her, but she doesn't answer, though he thinks he hears her whisper, faintly, just before she closes the front door, "No. Where *you* going?"

On the last day of the season, Charlie is wondering about a lot of things.

Fourteen years in the minors makes him a journeyman, and everyone on the team—especially the younger guys—knows that he's destined to be a career minor leaguer. It's way too late for the Majors to call him up.

But, just once, he thinks, he'd like to hit that home run.

His lifetime batting stats include a couple thousand at-bats, 443 hits, a batch of singles, 88 doubles, and 16 triples. He'd like to have just one number **1** in the column for **HR**. A *one* would look very nice and symmetrical there, he thinks as he drives to the game. A *one* would be just right. He's not asking for some crooked number, like a 5 or an 8; just a *one* would do. A straight line to somewhere. To the future, maybe.

He pulls his Chevy onto the crumbling asphalt parking lot and angles into his usual stall, third one from the left. The game's scheduled for seven p.m., he wonders if this will be the day. "If not today," he hears Coach Cy's voice echo in his head, "Then most likely tomorrow. If not tomorrow, then the next day. Or the next season. It'll all happen, eventually. Give yourself time. Give yourself a break." Coach Cy always had so much sense, so much good advice. Cy's sayings had wisdom and depth; the guy knew the history of the game, how it fit with the rest of the world, and Charlie was glad to be playing under him. No, not just glad— *proud* to be under the leadership of such a man. The man had a way of giving him encouragement, hope.

All spring and summer, Charlie has been religious with workouts; he's been weightlifting, trying to teach his muscles to grow stronger. He's been cranking out two hundred pushups a day; he's been on the Nautilus and the weight machines at the Y to build up his biceps and triceps and infuse them with power, even though Coach Cy advised, "Sometimes when you gain, you lose. More power, less finesse. More muscle, less grace. You realize that, don't you?" Coach's thoughts were often enigmatic, but always worth pondering. "Don't swing for the fences," Coach always said when Charlie was upset about never hitting one long ball. "Let the fences come to you."

As he sits in the idiling car a few minutes, his mind jumps again to Alicia's note that he found taped to his glove this morning. "It hurts to write this," the note read. "I'm so sorry, but I just have to have some time away from you."

The argument they had last night flashes through his mind. It started with the TV remote that was lost, and then escalated into other things.

"Everything's changing, Charlie," she said, a tear stinging her cheek. "*We're* not the same."

"But why? Why can't things be the same?"

"I don't know. Just a rule of the universe, I guess."

"What universe?" he asked, but she didn't reply to him. He heard a rumble of thunder outside the apartment. He pictured the chalk line on the third base side of the field, the raindrops pock-marking it at first, then pouring down steadily and blurring it. "*What* universe?" he asked again, his voice rising. She still didn't answer. "Damn it all," Charlie snapped, frustrated. "Coach Cy would tell me *what* universe. He'd say…"

"Coach Cy?" Alicia interrupted, exasperated. "Why are you always talking about some person named Coach Cy?"

"What do you mean?" He paused, heard the kitchen wall clock tick a few seconds. "He's our coach."

"There *is* no Coach Cy, Charlie. *You're* the player-coach of this team. So why do you keep talking about some Coach Cy?"

Charlie had no comeback. He just stood there, arms limp at his sides. That voice was so clear in his dreams, so vivid and convincing in his head, he started to think it was a real person. At that moment, he finally admitted it to himself. He realized Cy wasn't real, not at all—just a voice. A voice filled with riddles, hunches, guesses.

Now, Charlie clicks off the ignition, closes his eyes and just sits there while, hands clutching the wheel as if to stop it from turning. "I'm waiting for you, Charlie," he hears Alicia's voice say from afar. "It's your choice."

In the ninth inning, his team down by one run, a runner on first, Charlie hears his name blurt though the tinny speakers and echo across the field. There's a flutter of floppy applause from the small crew of hometown fans that have stuck with this team all season, a team that has mustered a meager second-to-last finish in the league.

Charlie steps over the line of the batter's box, and the thought crosses his mind: *What if I did step on that damn line? Would something bad happen? Or would I find out who I really want to be?* For an instant, he actually thinks he feels his heels edging toward the white stripe of chalk as he levels his bat across the plate.

Charlie knows this relief pitcher; he's faced him a dozen times before. A lanky 23-year-old, the kid was a standout with the Texas Longhorns in college and got signed quickly by the minors. Everyone says he'll be called up to Triple-A soon and then be the next rising star in the Majors. But Charlie knows the kid's tendencies, his idiosyncrasies, as pointed out to him once by Coach Cy. Charlie knows his first delivery will be a fast ball, knee high, clipping the outer corner of the plate.

And this time, Charlie will be ready for it.

He waits for the ball, his thin arms rotating and rotating the barrel of the bat as if stirring the sky. And for a moment, he believes he *is* stirring the sky. Or is it the sky, stirring him? He's not certain; he knows he'll just leave that mystery to Coach Cy. His wise voice always knew what to say in a situation like this. But that was in the past; right now, Charlie concentrates on what he must do alone: meet a round object with another round object in the exact spot, make wood fall in love with leather. Make leather fall in love with sky.

The scattered cheers of the hometown crowd go silent as he focuses, his fingers clenching the handle of the bat, unclenching it, then clenching it again. He feels the muscles in his arms ready to uncoil like a cobra. For a split second he pictures himself sliding his arms around Alicia, holding her tightly, letting her go, then hold her tightly again.

Charlie steps out of the batter's box for a moment to compose himself. "*It'll happen, kid. It'll finally happen,*" Cy predicted last night, just before Charlie fell asleep. Charlie replays Cy's farewell speech now, the way it poured out of him, the Zen-like words baffling but mesmerizing: "*It'll happen, sure as leather and wood, sure as the distance between what you know and what you don't understand,* Cy seemed to say. *Sure as earth and sky, sure as dirt and the pale expanding clouds, sure as silence and sound. Sure as a laugh or a cry. Sure as flying in the air or crashlanding on the hard bristly turf. Sure as sunlight and darkness, as what you've lost and what you've gained. Sure as knowing right where you are, your cleats digging into the soft, moist soil, and where you want to be. Sure as life and death, and whatever's in between."*

When Charlie steps back to the plate, the pitcher goes into a gradual windup, like an elaborate underwater dance. Then, with a quick motion that surprises the air, his arm rushes forward and he releases the ball. Charlie feels like his whole life has led up to this one moment.

He sees the red seams, rotating over and over each other as the ball slowly approaches. The baseball spins like some forgotten planet: a tiny, isolated sphere caught out there in the vacuum of space. *It's beautiful,* Charlie thinks, concentrating on just his own thoughts, his own voice inside the chalky hollows of his skull. *So beautiful.*

The ball comes closer and closer to him, making a hissing sound, and Charlie steps toward it, ready to whip the bat around with all his strength. Ready to see the ball ignite like flash powder, like a supernova exploding in space. Ready to feel its resonance travel through the bones of his wrists, through his forearms, and all the way to his heart.

Charlie swings, and as he does, he's swinging himself into the driver's seat of his Chevy. Steering out of the parking lot, he taps the accelerator, the same way he'd touch his toe on first base. He's turning left at the corner on Main, the way he'd casually trot around second base, then drives straight for two blocks, like a runner loping toward third. He pulls the car up at Alicia's apartment on Mulberry Street, clicks the ignition off. He can see the glow from her upstairs bedroom light, thinks he sees her face—smooth and oval—appear in the window. He loves that face; he knows it now.

Slipping off his cleats and socks, he jogs barefoot up the cracked sidewalk toward her front door, stepping on lines as he does, feeling the universe tilting, then straightening beneath him. His round trip brings him that amazing distance from the base paths to her front porch, where, not at all out of breath, he takes one last leap, landing gently, but solidly, on home.

THE WHISPER OF VINTAGE BASEBALL PHOTOS

I bought them in antique stores and kept them in a drawer: vintage team photos from the 1870s and 1880s where the players line up in two rows, their expressions stern, their eyes pale because they blinked several times during the few seconds when the photo was being taken. The players wear small-brimmed hats squared off around the edges, knickers, and baggy wool uniforms. Team names like Farm Supply Co., Ruby Legs, Pastime, or Haymakers scrawl across their chests. They pose with proud handle-bar moustaches, hand-sized gloves, and a few crisscrossed broom-handled or Wagon Yoke bats. They often anchored themselves in front of a painted Victorian backdrop scene of a stream meandering through a tree-filled countryside, as if baseball was a game played in a studio. I kept my childhood baseball photos taken by my father in that same drawer, stacked below those vintage photos. Today, I pause in front of the dresser and lift my hand to the drawer that, I hope, contains the one particular photo I remember so well.

That afternoon, after I made the Babe Ruth team, my father told me to step to the back yard in my new blue and white uniform. "Crouch in your batting stance," he told me.

"Where should I stand?" I asked, turning to face the sun.

"Not too close, not too far," he replied, knowing the range of our cheap Brownie camera.

I edged back a little toward the tall, dark-green pine tree that grew next to our house.

"Right there," he said, focusing on the small window of the viewfinder, the convex glass making my image appear curved.

Over the years, my father took several pictures of me, wearing my little league jerseys or Babe Ruth uniforms. Sometimes, when we looked at the photos—developed at a Rexall drugstore—the shadow of my father was visible. You could see his tall silhouette—thinner back then—stretched across the grass in front of me. You could see how he tried to hold the camera steady, his right elbow bent like a batter anticipating the next pitch.

Because the camera couldn't take high-speed photos, I taped a baseball to the barrel of my bat to simulate an action shot. Then I posed in my batting stance in front of the boughs of that big pine, my lips pursed, eyes intent on that leveled bat as if I was captured in mid-swing. In my mind, I pictured hitting a ball over a whitewashed fence into the Mrs. Fenske's yard beyond it. I envisioned an amazing stop-action picture, like the ones in the sports section when Ted Williams or Willie Mays stepped into a solid home run swing.

"Great," my father said after he snapped the shot. "That one'll turn out great."

But the pictures never did turn out that good. In them, I always looked washed out from the light, or blurred because he moved the camera slightly as he clicked the shutter. Sometimes, the top of the bat was cut off because the frame wasn't centered. And usually I was squinting into the sun, my eyes puffy, almost closed, my face pale over-exposed, a shadow from the bill of my cap slanting across my forehead. Worst of all, the edges of the masking tape showed beneath the ball, proving that it was a staged photo and not an actual hit.

Nothing was exactly the way you remembered it, or wanted it to be. That was the message of the baseball photos.

As the years passed, my father would steadily begin to lose his hair until he was nearly bald, and he'd work at a series of low-paying jobs that never panned out. He would let himself get out of shape and, unbeknown to all of us, begin to develop heart disease. As for me—in a few years, I'd become gangly and awkward, misplace my glove somewhere in a box in the garage. Senior year in high school, I laughed with my buddies as we sipped stolen beers and smoked Marlboros in the narrow space between the theatre and the hardware store. I fell away from the game I loved, and never played on a team again.

Those years, my father and I no longer had much to say to each other. Sometimes, when he'd drive us in his Chrysler to the hardware store to pick up some woodworking tools, we'd ride without speaking. He'd drum his fingers on the wheel at the stoplight, while I'd pretend to fiddle with the static-filled AM radio for a rock song that I liked or glance out the window as we passed the blurred jungle gyms on empty playgrounds.

But during my playing years, those baseball pictures were good enough; it was the best we could do. After Dad brought them home, I flipped through them excitedly, like prize baseball cards. Then I'd proudly label them on the back, in black pen, with my name and the date and the team I was on. After that, I pasted them into a scrapbook with Elmer's Glue or slid them into a white envelope and kept them in a drawer.

It's a drawer that I'm opening right now.

I'm lifting the photos out of the yellowing envelope and gazing at them, one by one. As they slide across each other, they whisper like dried corn husks. Finally, I find it: the photo from that day I made the Babe Ruth team, taken by my father, who's gone now.

That afternoon, as soon as he clicked the shutter, I was held there, always age twelve, forever in the middle of a home run swing, hitting that ball into my black and white future. And all the while, my father's eyes were watching me intently, hoping to steady me as he centered my image in the viewfinder. His dark shadow was there, too, on the grass—always stretching toward me, not too close, but not too far away.

END OF THE SEASON: TOUGH LUCK BALLPLAYER IN THE DIAMOND BLUFF TAVERN

His wounds are always on the inside—they're nothing you can see.

It always happened years ago, old Willie will tell you—in the high school playoff or a state championship game. As he sits in the Diamond Bluff Tavern, sipping a beer, the bottle slowly beading with condensation, he'll tell whoever's listening about the knee: One game, after he made a great backhanded stop at third, he pivoted, felt the whole world pop out of its socket beneath him. He swears he's never turned the same since, not even to look into his wife's eyes.

If you go to the tavern this Saturday night, you might intend to order a beer, hear the juke box playing scratchy songs, and chitchat with the bartender. But your main obligation will be to listen to Willie and nod. Your main job will be to buy him another High Life when he finishes this one, and then to say to him: "Go on. Tell me more."

When you do, he'll gladly talk about the elbow: on a long throw from right field to home, he heard his elbow shattering. "The sound of glass marbles clicking together," he says. There was no pain at first, he explains, "Just the sound. That damn sound." Then, a sudden stinging, as though a million bees just landed on his arm. He shakes the arm a little now, just to remind himself, to let the memory enter the bone again.

He pours the fresh longneck bottle into a glass, takes a sip. A mustache of white foam tickles his upper lip for a few seconds and then it's gone. He inhales a Lucky deep into his lungs, holds it there. When he exhales from the sides of his mouth, the wisps of gray scale the outfield walls of his temples.

He works his way up to the shoulder. He'll tell you how the ligaments pulled as he slid past second and tried to grab the bag with one arm. "That hug cost me," he says, half smiling, half grimacing. He tells you it made a sound inside his shoulder as if someone was tearing a thick paper grocery bag in half. He could swear everyone on the whole field heard it. But then the only sound was the ump leaning close to his face and bellowing Yer out!

"Ah, it's a life," Willie muses, shaking his head, "being an ex-ballplayer. It's a full-time job, almost."

You nod and listen, listen, though it's a little hard to hear his gravelly voice beneath the whine of Hank Williams and Patsy Cline on the juke box. It's hard to see his face in detail through the thickening haze from the burger-lined grill.

Still, you begin to think that maybe everything he says is true—the world doesn't end, doesn't end in a sudden apocalypse, doesn't explode all at once—instead, it falls apart little by little: tendon, hamstring, wrist, heart.

He'll muse that he might join the senior softball league one of these seasons. He'll tell you he might just have to settle for swinging an aluminum bat at that big ol' swollen softball, a ball that could never knock the wind out of the sky the way a baseball could, even if you tried a million years. "Soon as I heal, maybe," he assures you.

He pauses a few seconds, and inside that pause, your job is to imagine, beneath his skin, the old blood rushing to feed distant muscles.

Finally, he leans his portly body toward you, motions you in with bent fingers, and tells you a secret.

"The mind's the worst," he confides with a raspy whisper. "Injure that, and you're injured for life." He claims it's never really been the same since he stopped playing baseball. He'll tell you about the way, lately, his mind keeps rewinding those same scenes.

"Never the good memories when you're older," he admits. "Never the good ones. Sure, I used to think about those just after I quit. You know—the catches, the late inning heroics. But let me tell you something. The ones that hurt, they stay with you longest." His face is like melting wax, his features drooping as he nods at the lit Hamms beer sign behind the bar, the blue waterfall tumbling endlessly onto gray rocks. "Those are the ones. The ones that told you you weren't as good as you damn well thought. The ones that told you were losing it."

He licks his lips, gets a look on his face like someone who's starving, though you've just watched him eat a double cheeseburger and a big plateful of chili fries. He stands up, ambles to the juke box, drops in a couple more quarters. Your job is to wince through a few more songs, to hear their lonely love aching through the speakers. Your job is to watch him buy another long neck, waddle back to the scarred wood table, settle his weight onto the card table chair. He takes a few swallows of beer, pushes the half-empty bottle towards the middle of the table, then rotates his head toward you.

All night he's saved the story about the big game, and he's ready to tell you about it now. "It was thirty-six years ago," he begins. "A lifetime to some. But to me, yesterday." It was the championship game, last of the ninth, two outs, game tied, the hometown crowd on their feet. He stands, steps to the middle of the bar, the smoky air hugging him. He lifts his hands to the right side of his body, his fingers curling, knuckles whitening on an invisible baseball bat.

"I heard my name called through the speakers," he tells you. "I stepped right into the batter's box, kinda pawed at the earth with my cleats, glared at the pitcher, and, and then..."

Not an injury, this time, you hope, but something good: a home run, a double, a triumphant moment to win the game. The team rushing to cluster around him, all of them bobbing and leaping and patting him on the top of his head. It's not just your job just to listen anymore, to endure these stories—you want to know all about this one. You're hungry, and you really want to hear it. More than that, you want to be there.

You know by the faraway squint in his eyes that he's seeing it happen again, that his whole life depended on that moment. You find yourself leaning forward, anticipating the ending, the moment that's stayed with him all these years.

But his face goes blank a few seconds, his thoughts veering off the baseline. He strolls back to the table, drains his beer, then turns and eases the sweating bottle back to the bar as though sliding the handle of a bat into a dugout rack. And then, without another word, he limps out of the tavern, his past like a thick layer of bandages taped gently, gently around one knee.

THE DREAMS OF BATTING GLOVES

It was a small, light package, and I wondered what could possibly be inside it.

It arrived in the mail on my birthday from my 21-year old son. I removed the plain brown paper, flipped open the cardboard box, and discovered, wrapped in the layered clouds of white tissue paper, a pair of batting gloves.They were black leather—Mizuno, size XXL. Excited, I quickly slid them on; they fit just right on my big hands, hands that were already dreaming of taking a swing with them later that afternoon.

On the back of the glove's thumb was printed Vintage Pro. As I read the words, it occurred to me. That's me: I'm vintage, all right—but I'm far from a pro. Vintage amateur is more like it. And then a second, more sobering thought occurred to me: how many more seasons will I be able to use these well-made gloves?

I have to admit that, after years of playing baseball, I've slowed down somewhat. I don't play with a team any more. When I do go out for some hitting and fielding practice with friends, my reflexes seem to be a little frayed from wear: my swing is less quick and powerful, my legs turn rubbery after chasing down a few fly balls, and my eyesight has faded a little, so sometimes, from the outfield, the baseball flying toward me seems tiny as a grain of sand. The next morning after a workout, when I slide out of bed, I can almost hear my knee joints creak a little, the rusty hinges of a warped door that won't quite open, or shut. My wife claims she can hear the sound from across the room.

The seasons pass as though you're flipping quickly through a stack of vintage baseball cards. The seasons pass with their dust and rain, their summer storms with sudden gusts of wind that tear the black nets from batting cages and loosen the aluminum sign from outfield fences. Then there are the winter blizzards that pile against bleachers and backstops, the corroded wires sighing in pain as the icy wind slivers through them. Every once-new baseball field eventually gets ragged. Their fences begin to lean like hunched shoulders, their home plates—

gouged by cleats—turn pale beneath the glaring sun. And the less an evenly-groomed infield is used, the more the stringy weeds erupt from its baselines. It's the way of the things: Like some wild, careless creature, change encroaches every day with its teeth of rain and snow and wind, and it's impossible to stop.

But these batting gloves I hold in my palm—with their solidly stitched top grain leather—will last a long time. After all, their cardboard label boasts Improved Grip Durability, so no bat will slip from my fingers and cartwheel down the third base line. Their Motion Arc Line mimics movement of skin, the label says, so when I wear them, they'll be one with my hands. I'll feel them give my hands strength; I'll believe I can swing faster and more accurately than I ever thought I could.

Lately, when I go to a ball field for a workout, I carry my baseball supplies in a Forever 21 bag. It's a bright yellow plastic bag with black lettering. My wife thinks it's a little weird to do that, and I suppose it is: to keep old, grass and mud-stained baseballs, a sweat towel and a leaking bottle of Gatorade in a plastic bag from a store that caters to young girls. A bag that's supposed to hold pretty neon tank tops and Estee Lauder Color-Glo Lipstick and sparkling necklaces. But I noticed the store in a mall once, and I liked the name, and besides, the bag is waterproof, in case it rains during an outing. Sometimes, as I carry it, I contemplate the idea of what it might be like to be forever 21. Not 22, just 21. Held there, ageless. Foolish thinking, I know.

Once, on a field last year, I noticed that when a bat hits a baseball, it presses a distinct shape into the wood. But it's not a round circle, like you might expect. I know this because that afternoon, I hit a muddy, rain-soaked ball with a bat, and afterwards I noticed the mark it left. On the dry wood of the barrel was a symmetrical oval, like an eye, looking right back at me.

But right now I'm looking at these batting gloves. I slide them on, left, then right, feel them cling to my wrinkled skin. They're leather lovers, and they seem to whisper Don't let go. Don't let go. These gloves: I'm sure they'll make my hands agile; I'll be able me to grasp things I never could, no matter how far out of reach they are. These gloves: Even if I lose them in the grass someday, I know that, thanks to the compass deep inside my chest, I'll find them again.

Years from now, when I'm finally confined to the dugout, I'll pass the gloves on to my son. They might be stretched a little and frayed, worn thin in the place where the bat's handle rotated thousands of times against my left palm. Maybe a seam will be pulled loose, allowing the skin to smile through. But I'll pass them on, and he'll slip them slowly into his big hands, and they'll fit just right.

As he steps to the plate, I'll be bent behind the backstop, watching, my fingers curled in the wires. He'll lean into a fast ball, hit it a long ways, and then think: It's not the bat. It's not my muscles or my timing. It's the gloves.

Someday he'll have a son, a boy who, at a young age, will take a sudden liking to baseball. And one day the boy will discover the batting gloves, the fingers rounded, in the bottom of a musty canvas bag in the corner of the basement and ask: "Hey Daddy, can I try these on?"

"Sure," my son will say.

My hands. My son's hands. His son's hands. The young boy will lift the gloves from the bag, uncurl them from their dreaming. He'll slide his fingers into them.

And none of us will be surprised when they fit.

WHAT'S MISSING:
THE THREE THINGS, AND SOMETHING ELSE

1

I've come to understand that, in the small towns like mine, there are always three things near the center of town: a church, a cemetery, and a baseball field. These three things seem to repeat themselves: the church, where I'm careful not to break a red and violet stained-glass window with a hit that clears the fence and bounds toward it. The cemetery, where the old ballplayers go—a place bursting with flower arrangements over the brown dirt rectangles of fresh graves. And then there's the ball field itself, right there between the two.

That's where I am.

I'm Lloyd Thayer, the oldest player on the Meadowlake Mudhens, the local townball team. Somehow the years have passed me by, slowly, yet steadily, and as of this season, I've been on this squad at least fifty years. Or a hundred. Don't ask me how many. But after next Sunday, the last game of the season, I'm retiring from the team for good. It's not a day I look forward to—not at all.

"Don't worry," Adeline, my wife tells me, trying to settle me down. "Don't think about it. The day will just pass by like a warm breeze. And the sun will still come up the next day and look you in the eye." I appreciate her for saying things like that, though I don't really understand them. When you're an aging ballplayer, sometimes you can't quite tell which way the wind is blowing.

2

On the Mudhens, I'm the team philosopher. Some of the players call me the team guru. Especially when I look up into the sky and predict exactly when and where it will rain, and then comment with something like "A little rain won't kill us, boys. But lack of rain will." Or when I see a young player who's all upset because he lost his favorite ball cap somewhere and I'll blurt "Lose one, find two."

I always seem to come up with these sort of sayings—things most ballplayers don't say—and after a while, I've become noted for them. Back in high school, a million years ago, I used to read books by the great poets and philosophers, and maybe they've rubbed off on me. The last few seasons, at team meetings at the beginning of the year, and I came up with my usual head-scratchers like "There'll be more wins than losses. And even if we lose all the games, there'll still be more wins." I never stumble over words. The words just seem to come to me, like water over a falls, and I say them glibly, like I'm a baseball sage or something. Which I'm not. I'm just plain Lloyd Thayer, the oldest player on the Meadowlake Mudhens.

Lately, after the birthdays stack up like used paper plates after a church picnic, I've started to ponder my place in this world, and on a ball field, too, for that matter. "You think too much," the woman I love tells me. That's Adeline for you, always telling me what I do too much and not enough of. Adeline: she's a woman of noble heritage, and I'm just a peasant, working the field of second base. I'm just a humble man who should bow down to her, though I don't do that as often as I should. Still, I appreciate her suggestions, because in this life, sometimes you start doing a lot of one thing or not enough of another, and you don't ever question it, or ask yourself why. Adeline's my rain when I need it, when my soil is thirsty and so brittle you could bounce a leather ball high off it. She's my sun when I'm sopped and mired in mud, the afternoon game called because of wet grounds.

3

On the amateur team, my role is not speed, like it used to be when I was in my twenties. Back when I was twenty-one, I could chase down a hawk's shadow gliding across the vast expanses of the field.

My role is not power, like it once was when I could pop a hole in the blue balloon of the sky with a towering drive. When I was younger, I used to be able to hit a long one to left, and a few times it would clear the wire fence, bounce one, two, three times, and end up between the tombstones at the edge of the cemetery. The ball boy trudged out there to retrieve it between innings. "Sheese," he exclaimed as he brought the ball back, clean and white except for the one scuff mark on it. "Why do you keep hitting it *there?*"

So what's my role on the team these days, you might ask? It's agility. It's finesse. It's being in the right place at shortstop at the right time. It's learning about the batters so I know when they're going to hit the ball, and where. It's timing on the base paths. It's studying a pitcher, reading his fine print so I know his habits, such as when he brushed his teeth this morning, what radio station he plays in his truck, and exactly how he'll hesitate before begins his motion toward the plate. Lately my throws from shortstop are more about accuracy than speed, and that counts for something, especially if you're a base runner trying to score a run and realize—when you're still two steps away—that my throw from deep short is already nestled cozily in the catcher's glove.

And after the game, my role is to be agile with my words, leap-frogging here and there as I summarize the day's action. "We won, but we lost a little, boys," I might say, if it was an ugly game where we made a batch of errors. Or if we looked pretty good out there: "Yep, we're flying today. But we're grounded." Or, if we lost by a lot, and the guys are slumped on the bench with their heads down, I might turn to them, clap my hands together, and announce "You know, a tree has roots, boys. Even a tree cut down to a stump still has roots."

At home with Adeline, we talk. "How'd it go today?" she asks.

Feeling a little tired after a practice where I didn't do very well, I toss my jersey down the clothes chute and say "Not so great. Guess I'm a little like the rust on the fender of my pickup truck."

"No you're not," Adeline says, correcting me.

"If I'm not that, then what am I?" I ask playfully. We do this wordplay thing once in a while, both of us getting a kick out of it.

"You're more like the wheel that rolls over the rust. That's what I'd say."

"Oh. Okay, gotcha," I reply, though she's surprised me with her comeback once again. I thought I was the sage, the image maker, the baseball Buddha. And though I smile at her and nod, I have to think for a long time about what she means.

4

My hometown ball field is a place that's real as the sod beneath my feet, but at the same time, it's still sort of a metaphor for me. It always has been. It's an arena, a platform, an expansive green court where you risk your life, like in the ancient days of battle. A place where you prove that you can sink or swim, triumph or fall. It's the place where you show you can hit the ball harder, make the better catch, throw faster and further than your opponent. And if you lose, you die a little out there. That's what the field is all about, I used to think, though lately I've come to understand that it's not really as dramatic as all that. Instead, it's about sitting in the dugout before the game and glancing over at your opponents, who are doing the same thing, and then nodding at them as they nod back, as if each knows what the other must do, and, no matter what the outcome, each player respects—and forgives—his opponent.

It's as if each player understands three basic things: you might win, you might lose, but no matter what happens, you learn. That's what counts when you're a ballplayer: not the winning or the losing, but the learning. What you come back with. What you carry back from the field besides the surprised leather face of a well-hit liner. That's what counts. Not the numbers on a scoreboard, but a few good memories chalked up on the back of your brain that no one can ever erase.

And I can't help but dread the way those memories will be put on hold next Sunday, after my last game.

5

"Ever hear that whistle when the train passes the field?" I ask in the evening as I sit with Adeline on the sofa, watching the glow of the TV. Sometimes the Burlington Northern clunks past during the seventh or eighth inning of our night games.

"Yes. Why?"

"Sometimes I feel like the sound of that whistle." Adeline gives me an questioning look when I say that, so I add "You know—the way the sound sort of disappears in the darkness."

She clicks off the TV with the remote and the room goes dim and grainy. "Okay, Lloyd," she asks, her voice tender. "What's on your mind?"

"Let's face it, Adeline," I sigh. "I'm playing beyond my years. I mean, I ache all over after some games." The words look like dark shapes in the air as I say them.

"I know," she replies. She knows I won't admit my age to anyone.

"Sometimes, after a game," I confess, "It feels like there's broken glass inside my knee joints."

"Oh," she says, a soft sympathetic sound. "Sorry to hear that."

"Ah, hell. I should stop yammering so much. I sound like some scratchy old crow. Emphasis on *old*."

It makes her blink when I say this. After a long pause, she finally says "Lloyd, you've got to stop thinking of yourself so negatively. You've got to stop thinking of yourself as old."

"Then what am I?"

"You're not old. I mean…," She struggles for words, pursing her lips, which are pink, like fresh skin sealed over a scar. "You're not young either."

"So what am I?" I insist.

Her hands move in the air like the wings of a pale dove, and they brush back her auburn hair with the faint gray streaks weaving through it. "You're just somewhere in between."

I hate the in-betweeners, the short pop-ups that rise and float just beyond the infield and then fall quickly as I race back on my creaking knees. The sky lifts the ball, but it always lets it drop. It owns it only a few seconds, and caresses it up there, but like a child giving up his or her old toys, it eventually lets it go. And those soft, arcing hits always seem to fall a little short of my glove lately.

Being a ballplayer, at my age at least, things are always in-between. There always seem to be three things in my life: that church, sinking slowly into the ground, the cemetery, with its jagged-teeth tombstones that lean a little more each year, and the ball field, caught there between them, a green island in the middle. Lately I've started to suspect that there's something else. But what? I ask myself. What else is there besides stained glass and polished granite and a small ballpark?

Adeline knows, I suspect. She'd tell me if I asked her. But I don't. Lately I just keep the questioning to myself.

6

This week I've been picturing myself, walking into the dugout for my final game. My teammates might look up at me for some tidbits of humor or wisdom. "Hey Lloyd, what's the word today?" they'll ask. I hope I'll still have some things to say, a few witty comments they can latch onto, a couple of words to buoy them up. Maybe I'll say something like "We live and die on a diamond, boys. Not a twenty-carat one, but it's every bit as precious."

Maybe that will puzzle the twenty-year-olds with their iPhones in their back pockets, make them shake their heads or tip their ball caps way back on their foreheads. Maybe they'll chaw on their wad of bubble gum and give me a dumbfounded look, these young guys with so much of their lives ahead of them that they never think about the end. But a few players—the slightly older fellows—just let a faint smile cross their face and nod, as if they know what I mean, and then slide on their gloves, hop from the dugout and onto the waiting field.

7

"Lately I feel like a bird," I said with a sigh to Adeline the other night. "Like I'm flying against an oncoming storm." We were lying in bed; I had just finished paging through an *Outdoor Life* magazine, and she was reading a romance novel, the soft glow of the lamp falling across the patchwork quilt that rippled over both of us.

She placed the novel face down, pulled the quilt over her silky navyblue nightgown and up to her chin. Then she asked: "And don't you think everyone feels that way? You don't think I feel that way sometimes, too?"

8

Once I hit a long fly ball to the rotunda at the back of the church. On first bounce, it shattered a basement window. I told our pastor about it, of course, and offered to pay for it, but he declined, telling me to just add a little extra to the collection plate the next Sunday. The next week, when we came to practice, I noticed that the window had been replaced by clear Plexiglas. So it would be unbreakable, I figured. That Pastor Reginald always knows how to solve a problem. If a window is broken, he'll fix it, and keep it from breaking again. If a life was in danger, he'll rescue it. It was the way of pastors, I guess. The way of pastors was to make an impact on people's lives, just like the way of ballplayers was to make a dent in the grass beyond the outfield fence, or the aluminum scoreboard in center.

9

On Sunday—the morning of the last game of the season—Adeline and I walk up the gray stone steps to St. Cecelia's church for the nine o'clock service. We hear the soft organ music and sit in a wooden pew in front of the gold-leafed altar with the marble pillars. On this warm morning, it's already hot and humid and still inside this place—a place where I was baptized as a baby, my wails echoing from the domed ceiling, this place where the townspeople gather for funerals. The church usually feels solid to me with its thick walls and the plaster statues of saints gazing placidly at the congregation. People have said no tornado could ever rip through those granite-block walls, and they're probably right, since the church has been standing here since 1876. But today, I can't stop thinking about my last game, and the place doesn't feel all that secure to me.

As the pastor goes on and on about life and death and eternity, I notice the morning light streaming through the tall, arched, stained-glass windows. One beam of light angles right toward me, bathing my hands in purple. Purple, like my circulation is cut off by rubber bands. And for those few seconds, my hands, my whole body feels numb. I feel a sudden panic, and I'm not sure what to do. So I try to mouth a little prayer I learned as a kid, though it's been so long since I said it I can't remember all the words, or how it ends. Then I turn my head toward the stained-glass window and notice one clear glass pane at the bottom of it. Somebody must have broken that pane, and it got replaced. Still, through that clear pane, I can see the field. When I look through one pane to see the sheet-metal signs on the outfield fence glistening in the sun, the supple expanse of grass stretched wide and taut, it calms me down, and I feel okay again.

At the end of the service, Adeline and I—hand in hand—shuffle down the black and white tiled aisle of the church and exit through the heavy oak doors with the wrought iron handles. Outside, I squeeze Adeline's hand tightly for a few seconds. And then I let it go.

"Where you going, Lloyd?" she asks, but I don't turn to answer. The next thing I know I'm jogging across the parking lot. I'm running through the open gate of the cyclone fence and onto the infield.

I reach my spot at shortstop and, for a few seconds, I close my eyes and stand there in my white shirt, my striped tie and the loose dress slacks that don't quite fit. I imagine what's to come, later that afternoon. Picture, after the game's over, the sun beginning to set behind the railroad tracks that angle past the third base line, the red glow reflecting like rust off the tracks. Picture myself, tugging at my sweaty Mudhens jersey as if it's too tight or too loose. Picture myself, hooking my cleats on a chipped wooden peg, dropping dirt-stained socks that fall—in slow motion—into my duffle. Then I'd be standing there barefoot, listening to the southbound train trundle past. Listening to its whistle fade as though it's out of breath. Listening to a crow cawing on top of the light pole and the cicada click of cleats on the concrete dugout floor as—one by one—my teammates file past me to say goodbye. Picture myself silent, not saying anything back to them, all my words suddenly dried up.

I open my eyes and see Adeline, pushing through the gate. As she strolls toward me in her pale crème dress, I realize there are three things I know well about her: her deep and knowing gaze, her touch that feels like electricity on my skin, her voice, always clear and wise. Those are what make the most difference in my life; from those three, all other things spring. From those three things, all life begins. I come to her, like some castaway drifting on the sea for a long time. She's my island. It's always that way with her: in her presence, I step onto shore or crouch out of my cave, I evolve, I rise to my feet, I understand the tight spiral of my soul better.

She stops a few feet from me, a worried look surfacing on her face. "What are you doing out here, Lloyd?" she gasps. She knows it's only ten in the morning, and there's no game until two o'clock this afternoon.

At first I don't say anything. Finally I whisper: "I don't want to die. I just don't."

"Well you're not dying," she says quickly and firmly, the words hanging there a few seconds. "You're not."

"But some days, I mean…," I say, stumbling, "Today, I feel like…."

She puts her index finger over my lips, shushing them. Her fingertips are soft, and taste sweet—like vanilla hand cream—and I don't finish my sentence. I say no more, just stand there, feeling the breeze ruffle my shirt, feel it lift my red and purple striped tie for a few seconds before it lowers to my chest again. At that moment, time seems to stop.

It's then that I think about filling up the pause by muttering a clever sentence—one of my sayings, maybe. But I know this isn't the right time to be elusive, or to come up with some witty comparison. What I need instead is plain honest language. Words I should have been saying to her all these years. I've always believed in three things: the church, the cemetery, the field. But now I realize there's more than that; there's one more thing, something I've been overlooking.

Love's the other thing. She is. Like making that one catch I really need to, I reach out and wrap my arms around her waist. And that's when I begin, slowly, to tell her so.

CIRCLES: THE OUTFIELD DANCER

A veteran ex-ballplayer once told me this, though I didn't fully understand his words at the time, because I was too young. I don't remember exactly where he spoke to me. It could have been in a weedy back yard as we sat on lawn chairs in spring, listening to a ball game blaring from a radio perched in a half-opened window. Or maybe we were on the warped bench of an empty dugout, the dried husks of September leaves swirling around our ankles. The point was, when he spoke, his voice sounded like the deep baritone of my father's voice, a voice that's been gone now for a decade.

"All wise ballplayers know this," he told me. "Time keeps passing, and the world keeps rotating, like one huge baseball. Nothing can stop it from spinning, or from the way it orbits around the sun year after year. So don't forget to pause and enjoy the moments." His voice went silent, and he took a long, deep breath, held it, then exhaled. "Things change, and they don't change. But somehow the circles always seem to intersect. This might sound puzzling to you right now. But you'll see what I mean, eventually."

The circle came around to its starting point one Sunday morning last spring. It was Easter weekend, and my son—in his twenties and living out of state—returned to visit for a few days. He and my wife and I drove to a nearby ball field to play catch and hit a few fly balls.

With my wife standing behind the backstop, leaning her hip gently against the wires, I poised in the outfield, ready, flexing my well-worn Rawlings glove, waiting for my son to hit some fly balls. Though he's tall and thin, my son has surprising power, and can loft a baseball a long way, so I stood deep in center. He set two baseballs on home plate, then tossed the third one from his palm into the air and whipped his bat around. The ball jumped from the Louisville Slugger, a faint beige streak.

I squinted at it. The ball rose skyward, and about halfway into its trajectory, it suddenly vanished.

The sky was still there, but the ball—wrapped in the tissue paper of hazy blue—had somehow disappeared in it. I stood there helplessly a few seconds, wondering if he'd hit a short popup or a long fly. I wondered if the spinning sphere was headed right toward my blinking face. I realized that ball could strike me hard, sending sparks through my skull and leaving me with a black eye, a broken nose, or worse.

As if I knew what I was doing, I lifted my glove to the sky, poised it there, and, a couple of seconds later, heard the ball hit the ground. I turned around to see it taking an awkward skip at least twenty feet behind me.

At that moment I had a sudden flashback to the humiliation of my first little league game, when, having no idea where it would land, I misjudged the first fly ball that was hit to me. I gave my son a shrug, chuckled, then jogged to pick up the ball and threw it back to him.

Before his next swing, I swiped at my eyes with the sleeve of my T-shirt, thinking it would clear my vision. After all, I told myself, the cool morning air was making them water. Or maybe it was a fleck of dust in the corner of my eye.

On his next hit, I pretended to judge the fly ball, but again it faded from my view as if it had been swallowed by the sky. It landed a few yards from me with a thumping sound, a tiny earthquake shuddering beneath my cleats.

My son lowered the bat to his side and walked toward the pitcher's mound. "What's up, Dad?" he called, noticing that something was clearly wrong. He'd seen me make some nice catches in the outfield during my playing days. "Sun in your eyes?"

"Yeah, maybe," I called back to him, lying. Deep down, though, I knew; I knew that the baseball wasn't doing some kind of disappearing act; it was my eyes that were no longer seeing it. After a couple of decades of squinting at a baseball from deep center field, your eyes go bad. It's safe to say that nearsightedness and outfielding don't mix. Middle age and outfielding don't mix, either, though I still, of course, want to deny it.

As a kid, I never pictured myself as an older man, satisfied with spending my time fertilizing a groomed yard or doing handyman projects with a Skill-Saw in a garage or lounging in a La-Z-Boy and numbly watching TV. At age ten, I wanted only three things: baseball, baseball, baseball. And I pictured myself, older, maybe, but still on a ballfield somewhere.

I retrieved my son's second hit and threw the ball back.

As he stepped to the plate again, I reached down, plucked some blades of grass, held them in my palm. I let them spiral from my fingertips, studying them as if to check the direction of the wind, or to read a sacred message of some kind. I knew I could judge the wind; I was always able to do that. As a kid in little league, I could always catch the breeze in my open palm and tell if it was blowing toward right or left field, if it was stirring up a storm, or simply rippling the sky like the surface of a calm pool.

Suddenly the thought struck me that—almost without my knowing—the forty-some years of my life had fallen away like playing cards spilled from a table. And at that moment, the catches or drops didn't matter anymore. Nor did the winnings or losings streaks.

The only thing that really mattered was that I was there, on a field, the lips of the wind lightly kissing my face. As I waited for his next hit, I took a moment to appreciate everything around me: the groomed outfield—like Adam's grass in the garden—that smelled like aromatic incense. Cumulous clouds on the horizon, billowing like the whipping cream on top of the sundaes I savored as a kid. The distant bases on the infield, pale as hosts. And standing close to home, my dear wife and our son, the morning light angling toward them in shafts of gold. It wasn't a cathedral, or a religious shrine that surrounded me, I thought to myself, but something like it.

The only thing that mattered was that moment of love, that moment of inhaling a deep breath of the early spring air, holding it for a few seconds. I felt that rush of exhilaration entering my arteries, the tiny rivers of my capillaries, felt it branch all the way to my fingertips and toes and then back to my heart. Those were the things that mattered.

"Dad, you okay out there?" my son called, interrupting my meditation.

I replied with the only word I needed to say. "Sure," I called. "Sure."

So he tossed the third ball in the air, took a quick swing, the bat making a cracking sound that echoed back and forth across the field. As the baseball took flight, it seemed, to me, small and distant, like a photo of the earth from outer space. It was that far away. And that lonely. And that beautiful.

Later, driving back to the house, my son would make a suggestion. "Hey Dad, maybe you should just get some inexpensive distance glasses," he offered. "For playing, I mean." It was his way of hinting that he understood what was happening to me out there. My wife agreed, giving him a knowing nod from the passenger's side.

"I suppose I could," I'd replied, knowing I'd have to admit my weakness, get over my vanity and my lifelong stigma about wearing glasses. There probably would be bifocals on my face and a nerdy elastic strap around the back of my head the following spring when I jogged out to practice. Hands on my knees, I'd poise there in the outfield with more humility, and—hopefully—a clearer vision of what was spinning toward me.

That morning in April, as my son hit the third one to me, I hoped the ball—a sphere of light—would find its way to my glove, connecting the two of us. I knew it was the same kind of arc his young son would, someday, trace toward him as he stood waiting in the outfield.

Tipping my head skyward and squinting, I thought I spotted the ball, high overhead, and I popped my fist in my glove exactly the same way I did in the outfield on that first day of little league when I was seven. That day, like this one, I took a few small steps, circling beneath it, hoping to know exactly where the ball would fall back to earth.

From a distance, it might have looked like a lone fielder celebrating something as he did a kind of joyful little dance. Yes, that's probably what it looked like: a small dance in the outfield.

THE THINGS YOU LOSE:
AN ELUSIVE KIND OF LIGHT

When you're an older ballplayer, what you lose is not your old glove, that oil-softened mitt you used each season from little league to high school until its leather fused with your flesh. Even though it was left behind in a sagging box in the attic, or maybe forgotten on a dust-blown field somewhere, the glove is not what you lose.

What you lose is not that faded Honus Wagner baseball card, passed down from someone's dad, then traded from kid to kid on playgrounds. What you lose is not that valuable card, kept in a shirt pocket until your mother washed it, and the card disappeared, shred by fibrous shred, into the soapy water swirling down the basement drain.

What you lose is not that fat-barreled Babe Ruth model bat you stumbled on as you walked through the weeds at the edge of your neighborhood field. After you cracked the bat on an inside pitch, you pounded a nail into the thin handle, then circled it with masking tape, bandaging it like a broken ankle bone, and leaned it in its familiar corner in the garage. One day your parents moved to a different rental house, and then another, and piled the things from the garage into boxes, and those boxes into other boxes, and those boxes into trucks, and you never swung with that bat again. You think you've lost it, but what you lose is not that bat.

What you lose is not your *Little League Champs* T-shirt, a shirt that shrunk smaller and smaller each year, tightening its grip around your waist and shoulders, a T-shirt that sprung holes in front and back, holes that grew larger and larger as if the shirt were gradually eating itself alive.

What you lose is not that championship game you replay in your mind for thirty years. It's not that pitch you keep seeing, the pitch you should have hit, the baseball's seams always pink as stitch marks from a scar that won't heal. It's not that looping fly ball you should have caught, a ball that falls in front of you, sinking slowly, like a wish you didn't make, like a coin dropped just beyond your fingertips into a deep well. It's not those moments, though sometimes they circle painfully in your brain, like limping, injured dogs.

When you're an older ballplayer, what you lose is not that vacant lot where you played, a small field with a warped wooden board for a home plate and two worn spots in the grass where batters anchored their feet. What you think you lose is that small wood-slat fence at the edge of the field, and the row of pine trees, and beyond it, a field of tall grass that, as you stood there, staring, seemed to stretch across the plains and all the way across America.

What you think you lose is that sandlot field in the evening when you were seven. It was a place where fireflies rose from the deep grass and into the air, their tiny yellow lights blinking at you as you tried in vain to catch one in your cupped hand. Every few seconds, they'd light up, but always somewhere else. When you asked the man who walked by your side how fireflies can glow like that when they're only insects, he said he didn't know. It wasn't electricity, exactly, he told you, but a power we humans didn't understand, an elusive kind of light. As you walked home, he slid his arm around your shoulder and told you a story about how each tiny firefly is like the soul of a person.

That field is gone; an aluminum-sided rambler suffocates home plate. You still have memories, but they aren't what eat away at you little by little, they aren't the real things you lose. There will always be gloves and cards and T-shirts and games and fields. The real thing you lose is more important than any of those.

What you really lose is the person who took you to that field each day, the person who always walked by your side. What you really lose is that act of lifting your baseball in the stillness of late afternoon and tossing it across the blue air between you and your father. What you really lose is that game of catch, that arcing connection between your hand and his hand. For hours, the ball wove back and forth, sewing your palm, from a distance, to his. You can replace all those other things, but what you really lose is that.

Years after your father is gone, something tells you to walk at dusk from your house to an empty ballfield at the edge of town. At the field, you pause, seeing a few blinking lights above the grass. You believe your father could be there, in one of those faint, tiny lights—speaking to you in a flickering code you can't quite understand.

So you stroll toward the center of the field, surrounded by those tiny illuminations that glow brightly for an instant, then go dark, then glow again, but always in a different place. And though you know how hard it would be to catch one, you still reach out with your cupped palm. You reach out, as if you believe it would be that easy to grasp an elusive kind of light.

ABOUT THE AUTHOR

Minnesota writer and teacher Bill Meissner grew up in Iowa and Wisconsin and has been a lifelong baseball enthusiast and/or player. He is the author of ten books, including three baseball-theme fiction books: *Hitting into the Wind*, a short story collection, *Spirits in the Grass*, a novel, for which he won the Midwest Book Award, and *Circling Toward Home*, a collection of photography and writing, published by Finishing Line Press, 2022. He has played baseball in little league, Babe Ruth League, amateur league, and has written articles for the *Minnesota Twins Magazine*, *Minnesota Monthly*, and *Baseball Cards Monthly*, for which he interviewed such baseball stars as Nolan Ryan, Kirby Puckett, Ken Griffey Jr., Paul Molitor, Dave Winfield, and Don Mattingly. He lives with his wife, Christine, in St. Cloud, Minnesota and plays occasionally with a pick-up group called The Catch and Release Baseball Club. His son Nathan is a charter member. His Facebook author page is https://www.facebook.com/wjmeissner

www.ingramcontent.com/pod-product-compliance
Lightning Source LLC
Chambersburg PA
CBHW050339110726
47899CB00007B/2562